Julia's Story

Other books by Catherine M. Rae:

Brownstone Facade (SMP, 1987)

Julia's
STORY

Catherine M. Rae

St. Martin's Press

New York

Design by Susan Hood

Library of Congress Cataloging-in-Publication Data

Rae, Catherine M.
    Julia's story / Catherine M. Rae.
        p.   cm.
    "A Joan Kahn book."
    ISBN 0-312-02935-7
    I. Title.
    PS3568.A355J85   1989
    813'.54—dc19   89-30141

First Edition

10 9 8 7 6 5 4 3 2 1

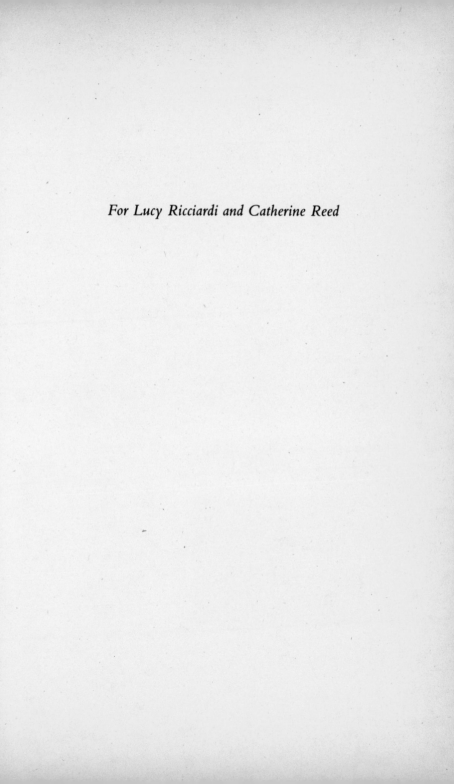

For Lucy Ricciardi and Catherine Reed

Acknowledgments

My thanks go to Lee and Dick Dunbar, to Vincent F. McLarney, and to Gene G. Rae, for their interest, their support, and their suggestions.

THE APARTMENT ON
MADISON AVENUE

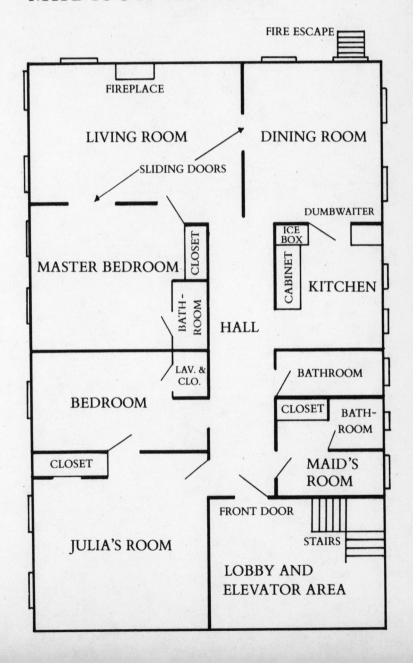

FIRE ESCAPE

FIREPLACE

LIVING ROOM

DINING ROOM

SLIDING DOORS

DUMBWAITER

MASTER BEDROOM

CLOSET

ICE BOX

CABINET

KITCHEN

BATH-ROOM

HALL

LAV. & CLO.

BEDROOM

BATHROOM

CLOSET

BATH-ROOM

CLOSET

MAID'S ROOM

FRONT DOOR

JULIA'S ROOM

STAIRS

LOBBY AND ELEVATOR AREA

Julia's Story

LEWISTON'S BOOKSHELF
129 EAST 59TH STREET
NEW YORK, N.Y.

June 8, 1952

Mr. Gilbert Hastings
223 East 76th Street
New York, N. Y.

Dear Gil,

Shortly before your sister Julia died last winter, she gave me the loose-leaf notebooks I am sending to you under separate cover. Annie, the maid who was with her for so long, and who has come to live with us, told me that Julia used to write in them at night when she couldn't sleep. I saw quite a lot of her during her last years, but until I read these pages I had no idea how difficult life had been for her at times.

I am not sure why she gave them to me; at first she said she thought I'd be interested in the section that deals with my brother Rob, and then she closed her eyes and whispered something about "safekeeping." I don't think her mind was quite clear toward the end, but it certainly was when she wrote about the Great Depression and how it affected all of us. She doesn't try to excuse anyone's behavior; rather she attempts to understand and explain the effects that the economic debacle had on us. She's so honest that sometimes it's painful. . . .

You'll notice that Julia divided her material into chapters; I can't

I

be sure, because I never discussed the matter with her, but it seems possible that she had a book in mind. You should have these papers, Gil; they belong to your family, not to me. And it's up to you to decide what to do with them.

I hope you are in good health, and that things go well with you. Bill and I are still running the bookstore Rob started so long ago, but we're beginning to think of retiring, possibly to East Hampton, where we still own the small cottage behind the big house we spent so many summers in when all of us were young. Remember?

All the best,
Ellen

1

Returning to live under my parents' roof was one of the most difficult and unpleasant acts I have ever been called upon to perform. I imagine it would be distasteful to any woman who has been mistress of her own household for a number of years, but at the time I had no thoughts to spare for other women; I was too wrapped up in my own misery. To make matters worse, I was not returning to the large, comfortable house on Seventy-first Street that I had known as a girl, and where no expense had been spared, but to a modest apartment on the corner of Ninety-second Street and Madison Avenue, with only one maid instead of the staff of servants we used to have.

I suppose I should have been grateful to have had any sort of roof over my head in the fall of 1930, when the depression that followed the Stock Market crash of the previous October was causing untold hardship across the country, but gratitude was not one of the emotions I experienced as I moved into the cramped and inadequate quarters assigned to me. Even today a feeling of bleakness, akin to despair, sweeps over me when I remember what led up to my arrival there.

★ ★ ★

When my parents were forced to sell the house we had lived in for so long—and it was only because of its prime location, just off Fifth Avenue, that a buyer was found—my father had some sort of breakdown, making it necessary for my brothers to take over his affairs. My mother did not go to pieces, but neither was she of any help. She simply assumed that someone, and it did not matter who it was, would see to things. She had been looked after, even pampered, from the day she was born, and confidently expected that condition to prevail throughout her lifetime.

Nevertheless, we all adored her when we were young; she was so beautiful then, and so good-tempered—I hardly ever knew her to be out of sorts. That came later. She was known to be a kind, generous person, one who responded readily to appeals for charity. I think that's why I found it so difficult to believe that financial reverses could bring about such a change in her. The depression did strange things to people —but more of that later.

By March of 1930, all the figures were in, and the outlook was discouraging, to say the least; aside from the income from a small annuity, about fifty dollars a month, my parents had nothing. The house was heavily mortgaged, and every penny Father could lay his hands on had been lost the previous fall with the collapse of U.S. Steel and Union Carbide, which he had been buying on margin accounts over the years. In a matter of days Richard Gilbert Hastings ceased to be a millionaire and became virtually a pauper. When the sale of the house was consummated the following spring, and it was obvious that provision would have to be made for my parents, my oldest brother, Rick, called a family conference.

Unfortunately he and I had never gotten along very well;

I must have been partly to blame, but for the life of me I cannot figure out what I might have done to cause him to treat me the way he did. I do not accuse him of actually disliking me; it was rather as if he merely tolerated my presence in the household, and would not have cared a whit had I disappeared. Perhaps I was a nuisance at times when we were children, I just don't know. It's sad in a way, because it could have been so different. I remember so well how I *wanted* him to like me. I remember, too, seeing him dressed in his first formal clothes (he must have been eighteen then, and I would have been eleven), thinking how handsome he looked, and longing for some sign of affection from him. It never came; even after I grew up, his attitude toward me, while invariably polite, completely lacked warmth.

Rick became a lawyer, a successful one. Immediately upon graduation from Harvard Law School he was offered a position with a Wall Street firm, and in a short time a partnership. I clearly remember the big party my father put on to celebrate that occasion, champagne, caviar, lobster, and all the trimmings; quite a contrast to the sober gathering that evening in March 1930, and in the very same room.

That was the last time we were all to be together in the drawing room of the old house, and it very definitely marked the end of an era. The large, gracious room itself, the scene of so much festivity, had undergone a change: the great crystal chandelier, ordinarily so highly polished and glittering, looked dusty and remained unlighted; the elaborate arrangements of hothouse flowers that customarily graced the half-moon tables against the walls were missing; and even the little silver candy dishes that used to be filled with wafer-thin after-dinner mints were empty.

Worst of all, the huge Persian rug that had been specially ordered for the room was gone, so that the parquet floor, while beautiful in itself, looked naked, bereft to those of us who were accustomed to seeing it covered. I heard later that Father had sold it to a dealer for a fraction of its worth. It was altogether a gloomy setting for that trying family meeting, with only a few of the lamps lighted and no cheerful fire under the carved stone mantel on the north wall, and it affected all of us. Except Mother, perhaps. I can still picture her as she appeared that evening in her pale-blue lace dress, sitting quietly in her favorite armchair, looking from one to the other of us with an expectant air.

"I don't know how Mother will react when she hears she'll no longer have a personal maid, Julia," Rick said softly to me as we waited for Father to finish his port in the dining room and come upstairs. "Eleanor thinks that will be the biggest blow to her."

"Just what arrangements have you made, Rick?" I asked, watching Eleanor as she leaned forward in her chair to catch something Mother was saying. I've always liked Rick's wife; she's not only beautiful, but also thoughtful, and she has one of the loveliest voices I've ever heard.

Rick did not reply at once. He turned over some papers he was holding and then looked up at me. "Wait until Gil and Margo arrive, Julia, and I'll spell it all out. But I'll tell you this much: we're all going to have to chip in; I'm counting on you and John to help. And I'll tell you another thing, which I do *not* intend to mention tonight: there's a substantial sum unaccounted for, a hundred thousand dollars, to be exact, which Father withdrew in cash from his account, ten thousand at a time, and there's no evidence that he used it to buy more stock. I can't figure out what the hell he did with it."

6

"Why don't you ask him, Rick?"

"Don't think I haven't. He just stares at me blankly and shakes his head."

"He must have lost it—" I began.

"And he's taken out whatever was in the vault at the bank," Rick interrupted. "Probably sold the jewels and whatever else was in there."

Just then my other brother, Gilbert, came in with his wife on his arm and hurried over to greet Mother. They made a striking couple; Gilbert had the matinee-idol type of good looks—regular features, dark silky hair with the slightest tendency to curl, broad shoulders, and slim hips. While he did not resemble my mother physically, he was like her in that he demanded rather than sought the good things in life, and his manner was such that his demands were usually met.

He was every bit as self-centered as Rick, but not as obvious about it, and so charming that one was apt to credit him with being more thoughtful and compassionate than he was. Gil could be fun at times, and I saw more of him when we were growing up than I ever did of Rick, but I don't think he cared very much about me one way or the other. In fact, I believe the only person he ever cared about besides himself was his wife, Margo, whom he practically adored. He got by on charm, not on brains; Rick was far brighter. It's too bad, in the light of what happened later on, that the three of us weren't closer. Oh, we did observe the amenities; in spite of there being no love lost between us we seldom had what Mother used to call "words."

As I watched Gilbert and his wife talking to Mother I had to admire Margo's poise. As usual, she looked stunning; her ash-blond hair gleamed in the subdued light and showed to advantage against the black of her simple but elegant dinner dress. She was nice enough, I suppose, but a bit too money-conscious for my taste, always wanting to know the prices of things. Aside from that, her main concern seemed to be the preservation of her slim (and very lovely) figure, which led her to attend all sorts of dancing classes. I've heard her carry on ad nauseam about the benefits to the body of interpretative, ballet, and even acrobatic dancing, but I prefer less rigorous exercise myself, like leisurely strolls through Central Park on sunny mornings.

"Is he coming tonight?" Rick asked, glancing around the room. "John, I mean."

"Yes, but later. He had to have dinner with a client, and he wasn't sure how early he could break away," I answered, suddenly wishing my husband were beside me. He had assured me at breakfast that morning that he would go along with whatever arrangements the family agreed on, but I did not relish the idea of making commitments without him.

"Ah, the clan gathers," Father said in a querulous voice as he came slowly into the room. "Who's missing? John Wilcox not here? Where is he, Julia? He shouldn't miss this—whatever it is."

He turned away, not waiting for me to reply, and sat down quickly in the nearest chair. Poor Father! Up until a few months ago, he had been a vigorous, active sixty-five-year-old, in excellent mental and physical health, but in that short period of time the changes in him had shocked us all. He seemed unable to concentrate on anything for more than a minute or two, leading me to wonder whether he hadn't had a stroke of some kind. Later on, when I asked Dr. Bronson if this could be the case, he said it was indeed a possibility, but since he had not been called in at the time, he couldn't say for sure.

Father had lost weight, too. He'd been a big man, tall and broad-shouldered, heavy without being fat, a good golfer and a splendid horseman. He was the kind of man who easily and naturally dominated any group in which he found himself (at least he had in the past), and as I watched him that night I found myself remembering how when I was a child I'd lie in bed chuckling to myself when I heard his deep voice and hearty laugh ring out above the noise of a party in the rooms two floors below—but that was long ago.

As Rick consulted Gilbert about some item on the papers he held in his hand I continued to observe my father, trying not to appear to be staring at him. Yes, I thought, he's definitely losing weight; the Queen Anne chair in which he sat, and which he once filled comfortably, now looked far too large for him, and instead of sitting erect and taking charge of the conversation he leaned his head against one wing of the chair and closed his eyes. He did not look well at all; his face, ordinarily so pink and white and scrubbed-looking, was lifeless, almost gray, and his thick white hair lacked its old luster. I think I knew then that he wouldn't last much longer, but of course I had no idea how difficult the rest of his life would be, for him and for me.

As Rick began to speak, Father opened his eyes and sat up straighter; he did not interrupt as my brother talked, which was unlike him, but gave the appearance of listening attentively to the plans that were being made for him. I guess he realized he was in no position to make them himself.

"I think you'll like the apartment we've found for you, Mother," Rick was saying. "It's bright and cheerful, with windows on three sides; you can see the Reservoir in the park from the dining room, and there's a large living room facing east and south. Also there are three good bedrooms. Only one maid's room, however; but since we can't afford more than one in-help right now—"

"No cook? No butler?" Mother asked in a surprised tone.

"We'll find you a cook who can serve at table, too, Mother," Gilbert said with a smile.

"And my own maid," Mother persisted. "What about her? Enough of the help has been dismissed as it is!"

"She'll have to be that, too, Mother," Rick said quickly. "You see, there's practically no money. Gil and Julia and I will have to whack up the rent and the maid's salary. What little we realize from the sale of this house, and any jewels and valuables—"

"Not my jewels, Rick! I can't part with them, ever!" Mother stood up and prepared to leave the room.

"Wait a minute, Mother," Gilbert said gently, putting his arm around her and urging her back into her chair. "We haven't finished—"

"No, we haven't," Rick said. "Whatever money comes from the sale of things" (I noticed how careful he was not to mention the jewels again) "plus the income from Father's annuity, should be enough to cover living expenses, at least for a while. If it turns out that there's some left over, and we can find something that will give you a decent return, we'll invest it—"

"No!" my father shouted. "No investments!"

"All right, Father, all right. In that case, we'll just draw on it as needed." Gilbert's tone was conciliatory.

"And I'll be the one to do the drawing," Father said angrily. "Who do you think you are? Just because you work in a bank—that doesn't mean you can tell me what to do with my money!"

"And I don't want to be told to sell my things," Mother

whined. "I don't see why I should have to. If we must move, we'll take everything with us, everything."

Eleanor, in response to a look from Rick, leaned over and spoke to my mother in a low voice, saying that of course she'd have all her favorite pieces with her, and that she, Eleanor, would help her arrange them in the apartment.

"You'll be much more comfortable there than you think, Mrs. Hastings, with all the rooms on one floor, and no tiresome stairs to climb."

I don't think it was so much what Eleanor said as it was her placating voice that calmed Mother. In any case, she sat back quietly and said nothing further about her "things." I hadn't realized until that moment how important possessions were to her—stupid of me, after having spent twenty years of my life with her. Father, too, was quiet after his outburst; he stared fixedly, if somewhat vacantly, across the room at the gilt-framed Venetian mirror he and Mother had brought back from their honeymoon. I was startled when he turned his head suddenly and saw me watching him, and although he looked away immediately, I caught the changed expression in his eyes. They were no longer vague and empty, but furtive, or I might say scheming or even crafty; completely foreign to his usual forthright, determined look. It worried me.

I hadn't ever been close to my father, but I liked him, and I'd never been afraid of him, as so many had. Over the years he'd been kind to me, generous too, and gentler than he'd been with my brothers. I suppose being the only girl in the family, as well as the youngest child, had something to do with it. But just the same, what I saw in his eyes that night sent a tremor of fear through me, and I was uncomfortable for the rest of the evening.

I don't believe I fully recovered my composure until John came for me and we were walking back to our apartment on Park Avenue, my arm tucked safely through his. He had spent a few minutes talking to Rick and Gilbert, agreeing readily to contribute to the support of my parents, although I knew he was concerned about the falling off of business in his law firm. Also, we had lost a fair amount in the market ourselves, as a result of which I had let one of the maids go, and we had canceled a trip to Scotland for the coming summer, choosing instead a less expensive vacation in Canada.

As we walked I told John what had gone on at the meeting, and when I mentioned the hundred thousand dollars that Rick could not trace, he sighed and shook his head.

"There are any number of things your father could have done with it, darling. He could have lost it gambling; he must have been trying desperately to recoup, you know; or he might have had some transactions he wanted to keep hidden. Who knows? Maybe he has it safely stowed away and isn't saying anything about it."

"Rick says it doesn't do any good to ask him," I said as John unlocked the door to our apartment. "I just hope if he did hide it he remembers where he put it. He's acting so strange lately; do you think his mind is going?"

"I don't know," he answered. "He looked pretty terrible tonight, but other than getting him to see a doctor, there isn't much we can do." He closed the door and shot the night bolt, and after we had hung up our coats he turned and caught me in his arms, pulling me close to him.

"I hate to see you so worried," he said softly. "You shouldn't be. Look at me, dear; let me see you smile. There! Did you know that you're more lovely than ever? When I went into that drawing room tonight and saw you standing near the window, my heart leapt the way it did the night I met you. Oh, my darling . . ."

I don't know why I didn't tell John about the furtive expression I saw on my father's face; I never kept things from him. I guess I might have mentioned it once we were in bed, but that night he made love to me so tenderly that everything else went out of my mind. It was a night to remember, for more reasons than one.

2

I won't soon forget the troublesome and trying weeks that followed the conference in the drawing room; not only were there countless details connected with the move to be attended to, but also hanging over us all was the ominous cloud of impending financial disaster. Prices on Wall Street were still falling, brokerage houses were closing, banks were in trouble; and everywhere the talk seemed to center on business failures, suicides, unemployment, breadlines, and the like. Perhaps it was just as well I was so busy with family affairs during that dark, nervous period—I had less time to worry about the total effect of the economic debacle on us.

Also, clearing out the old house was a sad business, sadder than I had anticipated. I have never considered myself a sentimental person, but I did experience a certain amount of nostalgia as I came across objects that reminded me of the luxurious upbringing we had all had. I lingered a few moments over the gold-plated fixtures in Mother's bathroom, the elaborate canopy on her Louis Quatorze bed, the sweet little sofa in front of the fireplace in my own deeply carpeted bedroom—all symbols of the wealth and ease we accepted as our due, now to be abandoned along with the way of life they represented.

And then there was the effect of the move on my parents; I couldn't help but feel a pang when I saw the wistful expression on Mother's face as she watched some of her favorite pieces being taken off to be sold or auctioned. One afternoon I found her huddled over in the rocking chair in her sitting room, crying quietly. When I put my arm around her frail shoulders she caught one of my hands in hers and leaned against me. A moment or two later she heard Father shout an order to one of the packers, at which point she straightened up, blew her nose, and asked me to send for a cup of tea.

To everyone's surprise Father took an active part in the preparation for the move, ordering cartons and boxes, supervising some of the packing, and making lists of the contents of the containers. It wasn't like him to show an interest in household affairs, but as Eleanor said to me one day when she and I were sorting table linen, he had been accustomed for so many years to directing operations in offices and boardrooms that it was not at all unnatural for him to go on exercising authority.

Eleanor herself was a tower of strength throughout the upheaval, coaxing Mother along, gently persuading her to leave for the auctioneer the more massive pieces of furniture that would never have fitted into the living and dining rooms of the apartment. Finally, by the first of May, the house stood empty, ready for the decorators the new owners were to send in, and my parents were established, albeit unhappily, in the apartment at Ninety-second Street and Madison Avenue. In spite of all our care, though, they had kept far too many of the possessions that had surrounded them for so many years, with the result that the apartment was woefully overcrowded and made to look smaller than it actually was.

It was unfurnished when I first saw it, and I remember thinking at the time that it offered plenty of room for two people and a maid to live in comfortably. It was at the top of a six-story building that had only ten apartments, two to a floor, the street floor being given over to small shops. As Rick had said, there were windows on three sides, making all the rooms light and airy, not caves like the ones in so many buildings. The only darkness was in the long, extremely narrow hall that led from the front door, past bedrooms, bathroom (the master bedroom had its own bath), and kitchen to the living and dining rooms at the southern end of the apartment. And Mother made that hall even narrower by filling the available wall space with cabinets and sets of shelves, all crowded with bric-a-brac—music boxes, figurines, pieces of Dresden china, that sort of thing.

Once they moved into the apartment, my parents' personalities changed startlingly, and not for the better. When they weren't querulous, they were silent, glumly silent. I don't know which mood was worse, probably the latter, because it seemed accusing—as if we younger ones were responsible for their misfortunes. At least that is how it struck me, and it hurt me, too, because any accusation like that was so undeserved.

We soon became accustomed to hearing about the shortcomings of the new residence: the living room was too small, the bathroom fixtures second-rate, the closets inadequate, and the gas fireplaces poor substitutes for the real thing. I tried to sympathize, but after a while I stopped listening to these complaints during the weekly visits that had always been, and still were, expected of us. I imagine the others stopped their ears, too.

We were all, Rick and Eleanor, Gilbert and Margo, and John and I, scrupulous in paying our respects, and tried to drop in on the discontented couple on different afternoons or evenings. That did not always work out; sometimes four of us would be there on a Sunday, and then no one until the following Friday. But when I tried to set up a schedule, Margo protested that she wouldn't know what might come up to prevent her from visiting on her day, meaning, of course, that she would drop in on her husband's parents only if she had nothing better to do. I didn't blame her too much; sitting in that overcrowded living room for forty-five minutes trying to entertain two unresponsive old people was not the most pleasant of occupations. I'm just as glad I have no children to come and pay dutiful visits to me when I'm old and decrepit. . . .

It seemed as if we had no sooner settled Mother and Father in the apartment than it was time to pack them up again and transport them to the summer house in East Hampton. Rick had wanted to sell that property, too, but Father made such a fuss that he desisted. Probably it was just as well, as things turned out. The house, though not without charm, would not have brought much money then anyway, since real estate prices were deplorably low. Also, a summer in the city in those pre-air-conditioned days would have added immeasurably to the misery of my already discomfited parents. They belonged to a generation to whom the thought of spending the hot months in New York was anathema; consequently, all of my summers up until 1915 had been spent out near the eastern end of Long Island. After my marriage, though, I stayed in town until John could take his vacation, at which time we went to Europe or wherever we pleased. Father, who loved a full house, tried hard to lure me into spending at least part of the summer in East Hampton, arguing that the heat and dust of the city were bad for my health, that John could come down for long weekends, that the country air would do him good, too, and so on. I did not go any more frequently than I had to, though, just for a special celebration like Mother's birthday, or the Fourth of July.

Eleanor was different; she and her two daughters spent several weeks with my parents each year, and if I remember correctly, sometimes the whole summer. Margo never went if she could help it; her parents summered at their large farm up on the Hudson, where she was needed, she said.

Rick and Gilbert were either unable or unwilling to drive my parents out to East Hampton that year. I overheard Gilbert say that he would feel like a fool driving a car that should by rights have a chauffeur, and perhaps, given his character and upbringing, one can understand his feelings. We had been accustomed to limousines all our lives; for a long time Father had a car and chauffeur for himself, so that the second car could be at Mother's disposal. It was her chauffeur who drove us to our private schools in the morning, and picked us up in the afternoon, and I remember that when I begged to be allowed to walk home with some of my friends, permission was refused; it might not be safe, was the reason given.

So it was up to John and me to take charge of the summer exodus. The day we left New York with Mother, Father, and Annie O'Sullivan, the maid, in the car with us was rainy and cold, unusually cold for June, and the long trip (there were no expressways or broad highways in those days) tired us all. Fortunately the big La Salle, with the chauffeur's compartment separated from the passenger area by a glass panel, was large enough to accommodate the five of us and the luggage fairly comfortably, but oh, how different it was from the departure from the city in earlier years! Then three or four servants had been dispatched several days in advance to open up the summer place, to air the bedding, launder the curtains, tend to the grounds, and have all in readiness for our arrival. We would travel in the old-fashioned luxury of parlor-car seats on the Cannonball, the express train to the Hamptons. Everything—tickets, luggage, even refreshments —was taken care of for us; all we had to do was curl up comfortably in the big velvety swivel chairs and enjoy ourselves.

As John drove slowly along the wet surface of the narrow road that ran between tracts of land covered with scrub oak and pine from Riverhead to the south shore of the island, I found myself thinking about the poor servants of my grandfather's day. They, according to the story, were sent out to East Hampton days ahead of the family in a horse-drawn wagon laden with trunks and supplies. We were told it took them two days to make the trip, and that they always stopped at the same boardinghouse in Smithtown for the night, where they all slept in the same room, and were given only such food and drink as my grandfather ordered for them. (He was a wealthy man, too.)

It was late in the afternoon when we pulled into the narrow lane opposite the cemetery on the village green and approached the house. This time, of course, no preparations for our arrival had been made, and in the gloomy twilight the almost derelict appearance of the place caused my heart to sink. The hedges needed trimming, the grass had not been cut, and I could see that at least two of the shutters had come off their hinges and were dangling drunkenly in the wind. Such a dismal welcome . . .

Once inside, however, I felt better; the rooms had a musty

smell, and needed a good cleaning, but they were dry, and seemed to be in order. Mother and Father sat close to the blaze John built up in the huge stone fireplace at one end of the large living room, she staring idly into the flames, waiting to be waited on, and he sipping a drink poured from the flask he had in his pocket. I left them and hurried upstairs to see about the beds. The sheets felt cold and slightly damp when I took them from the linen closet, but I used them anyway, hoping nobody would notice. After making up four of the dozen beds, setting out towels, and unpacking one of Mother's suitcases, I went back to the living room. My parents still sat where I had left them, and they looked so tired and old that I wondered how they would get through the summer in that large, empty house with only Annie to call upon. Poor Annie; she had come to us when I was a child, "right off the boat," as they used to say about the Irish girls. She'd started in as scullery maid, and over the years had worked her way up until she knew just about all there was to know about running a house, although she had never been promoted to housekeeper. When I asked her if she'd be willing to move to the apartment and work for my parents, her reply touched me.

"Sure, and I don't know where else I'd be going, Miss Julia," she'd said, relief evident in her tone. "I was wonderin' if you'd take Cook or who to do for them. I wouldn't have known where to look for another place—yes, yes, I'll do it, and gladly."

She produced a remarkably good dinner from the box of supplies we had brought with us, but in spite of the excellence of the food the meal was a dreary affair. John and I made several attempts at conversation, but since neither of my parents responded, our efforts went for naught. After a while the only sounds to be heard were Mother's sighs and an occasional grunt from Father. I think he must have had several drinks from that flask of his.

We had almost finished our coffee when Mother gave a slight start.

"Oh, dear," she said softly, "I knew I forgot something. I left Ben's picture on the table next to my bed! How could I have forgotten that?"

"I'll mail it to you, Mother, as soon as I get back to the city," I promised.

"But I don't like being without it! I always sleep with it beside me," she protested tearfully.

My brother Ben, who was killed in the battle of Château-Thierry, had always been her favorite, and she had never become reconciled to his death. He had been close to me, too, unlike Rick and Gilbert. He was only a year older than I was, and consequently we had been thrown together a great deal as children. Mother wasn't the only one to dote on Ben; almost all of the young women in our circle vied for his attention, and with his charm and good looks, who could blame them? Grace Millerton won him; they were engaged to be married when he went into the Army, and we were all looking forward to an elaborate wedding upon his return. Grace—I always liked her, and still do—married well. Ned Cochrane was known to be extremely wealthy, and from what I've heard he's held on to his money. I did think she married him rather suddenly, though; there was just an announcement in the *Times*, no big wedding or reception or anything like that. Probably her sister Rose's murder that winter was the reason; there was something peculiar about that, and we never heard the whole story. I sometimes thought Mother believed Grace should have remained faithful to Ben's memory; why else would she frown and tut-tut every time her name was mentioned?

In East Hampton that night my mother was quite unreasonable, insisting that she wouldn't be able to close an eye unless she had the picture of Ben next to her. I was unsuccessful in comforting her, and Father was no help at all; he left the table without a word as soon as he finished his coffee and went back to sit by the fire. In the end it was good, kind Annie who took Mother upstairs and tucked her into bed. All in all, it was an inauspicious start to what proved to be a dreadful summer.

3

John took the morning train back to the city the next day, and although I hated the thought of staying in East Hampton without him, I knew I would feel guilty if I left before seeing that the household was in order and making sure that Annie could cope. So I drove him to the station, reminded him to mail Ben's picture at once, and almost cried when he kissed me good-bye. He made me promise not to stay away any longer than was absolutely necessary, and I drove slowly back to the house, trying to make some plans for the care of my parents for the coming months.

I figured that if Eleanor brought the children down for a few weeks, or maybe longer, July would be taken care of, and if Gilbert and Margo could be persuaded to spend a weekend or two in August, the summer might not be too lonely for my parents. And I would feel free to go to Canada with John as we had planned. But I was not looking forward to the next two weeks. . . .

As it happened, I was not nearly as unhappy as I had thought I'd be. For one thing, the weather cleared up, making everything seem better, and for another, I was too busy to think about myself. I helped Annie with the heavy cleaning, washed windows, shook out rugs, swept the stone terrace, ran countless errands, and tumbled into bed exhausted at night. The days slipped by, and after I had made all the arrangements I could think of—with the butcher, the grocer, the milkman, the boys to cut the lawn (the gardener we used to have was far too expensive)—and found someone to fix the shutters, I began to think about leaving.

I tried not to let little things bother me, but I was heartily sick and tired of the incessant complaints of my parents about what was lacking for their comfort. Neither of them would face up to the fact that there was very little money, and that they would have to do without most of their former luxuries. Father resented having to give up his membership in the Maidstone Club, and Mother retired to her room to sulk when I refused to drive her over to a specialty shop in Southampton so that she could buy a summer wardrobe.

"They'll never understand that the money's gone, Rick," I said when my brother phoned one morning. "I think you'd better come and lay down the law before they run up a bunch of bills. They won't listen to me. They think I don't know what I'm talking about."

"I'll try, Julia," he replied, "but I can't get away just now. I have your letter about visiting over the summer, and I've talked to Eleanor. She thinks she can manage to be there for most of July, and I'll see Gil and see what he'll do."

I did not mention it then to Rick, but I was becoming more and more concerned about my father's surreptitious drinking; not that he staggered around the place or anything like that, but whenever he was near me I could smell whiskey on his breath. He must have brought a supply with him, because Prohibition was still in effect, and he couldn't buy any liquor in the village—unless, of course, he had a bootlegger. I suppose he had seen to it that whatever was left in the wine cellar of the old house had been transferred to the apartment, although where he'd hidden it I did not know. But Annie knew; when I asked her if she had ever seen any liquor in the apartment, she gave a little laugh as she went on shelling the peas and then looked up at me.

"Under his bed, Miss Julia, under his bed, in those special flat boxes. I've orders never to clean under there. Precious documents, he said, not to be disturbed. But I know. Tell me, now, is there a bit of mint in the garden? 'Twould go nicely on these peas."

I knew there had always been a mint bed near the fence that ran along the back of the property, and as I went to look for it I was reminded of a particularly lavish garden party my parents gave one year, in 1925, to be exact. I'm sure of the date because John and I were the guests of honor, the occasion being our tenth anniversary. Father loved a big party, and was in his element that day. I remember even now how expansive he was, moving about the terrace and lawn among the fifty or so guests, extolling the merits of the mint juleps that were being served. I overheard him boasting that he had found the only bartender in the state, maybe in the nation, who knew the proper way to make a julep, and saw him guide a small group over to the table where a cheerful-looking black man in a white jacket was crushing mint with a wooden pestle.

"Great quantities of fresh mint, lots of ice, lump sugar, first-rate whiskey, and plenty of elbow grease, that's all it takes," Father said, accepting a frosty glass from the smiling bartender.

No one asked him where he obtained his "first-rate whiskey"; at least I did not hear anyone inquire, but as I picked a few sprigs of the aromatic herb for Annie I thought of the rough-looking men who would appear from time to time (always at night) at the back kitchen door. And I remembered being quite startled one summer evening at the sight of two fishermen moving quietly across the lawn. A fog had come up suddenly, and I had been sent out to look for a sweater Mother said she'd left on one of the garden chairs. I stood still and watched the two figures approach the light that streamed out through the screen door. A moment later Father appeared, and the three of them moved off into the shadows.

They came on several occasions, and Father would always go out to see them, even if it meant interrupting his dinner. He was never gone long, and invariably reappeared at the table looking pleased with himself, but we knew better than to ask any questions. One night in particular stands out in my memory: we were all there, Rick and Eleanor, Gilbert and Margo, and John and I, for the weekend of Mother's birthday. We were at the table, with Mother looking almost regal in a flowing chiffon gown (Worth's, I think), and wearing the sapphire-and-diamond necklace Father had given her. We were just starting on the main course when one of the maids came in and whispered to Father. He had been denouncing President Coolidge for giving financial aid to the farmers, but instead of scowling at the interruption he excused himself and went quickly through the swinging door to the kitchen. When he returned a few moments later, we were engaged in what we hoped was a lively conversation about plans for a picnic on Shelter Island the next day, but I'm sure it all sounded forced. Why did we feel we had to give the impression of being oblivious to Father's actions? Because it was expected of us, I suppose.

"Obviously it's booze, darling," John said to me later when I told him I was puzzled. "East Hampton is a perfect spot for the rumrunners to unload their liquor."

"But how—"

"It's this way: ships flying foreign flags stand out in the ocean beyond the twelve-mile limit—it used to be three miles, but the government changed that—and anyone with a fishing smack or some other small craft can go out and stock up on whiskey. Costs money, though."

"And Father buys it from the fishermen—"

"Yes, he has an arrangement with one or more of the runners."

"But, John, isn't it illegal?"

"Strictly speaking, no. Not what your father is doing. It is illegal to manufacture, transport, or sell alcoholic beverages, but it is not against the law to purchase them. Your father is not breaking the law, darling, but he's probably dealing with some pretty shady characters—no, don't worry, darling. He knows what he's doing. Come on, love, we're wasting time. Get into bed."

All that came back to me as I made my way to the kitchen with the mint for Annie, and I wondered if illegal whiskey was still being smuggled into the coves and inlets that abound out near the tip of Long Island. I hadn't seen any sign of strangers since we arrived, but nevertheless I began to feel a little bit apprehensive. And to wonder about just how much my father was drinking.

The next time Rick called (I should say here that there is a tiny "telephone room," not much bigger than a closet, under the front staircase, so I was reasonably sure my parents did not overhear my conversations), I told him what Annie had said, and asked him if he thought we ought to get rid of the liquor in the apartment.

"Don't be stupid, Julia! He'd kill us if we touched it!" Rick was horrified at the very suggestion.

Why, for all his bluster he's still afraid of Father, I thought as I hung up the receiver and prepared to go out and cut some roses. As I was arranging the sun-warmed, fragrant blooms in the big cut-glass bowl that always stood on the round table in one corner of the living room, I wondered if it was the same with Gilbert, if he still feared the parental wrath. Father had often been pretty hard on the boys when they were growing up.

As I said earlier, I was never afraid of him, and when he brought up the subject of membership in the Maidstone Club again the next day, I simply left the room. Suddenly I'd had enough. I went over my lists once more, checking to see that I had taken care of everything, and then called John at the office to tell him I'd be taking the train back to the city the next afternoon.

"I'll meet you at Penn Station, darling, and then we'll go someplace and celebrate your return," he said, and I knew from his tone that he was as anxious to have me in his arms again as I was to be there.

I waited until after dinner to tell my parents I would be leaving. They were not at all pleased; Mother said she didn't know how they could get along by themselves, and Father accused me of being an ungrateful daughter. My assuring them that Annie had been fully instructed about running the household did little good, but they cheered up a bit when I said that Rick and Eleanor would be down soon.

"How soon?" Father demanded—and snorted when I couldn't say exactly when.

Strangely enough, or maybe not so strangely, neither one of them had a word of thanks for what had been almost a fortnight's hard work for me, although Mother smiled quite graciously when I kissed her good-bye the next day. I left wondering where I had failed them.

4

There are times when I find it difficult to rid myself of the thought that if we had taken our vacation in East Hampton that year, as my parents wished us to do, instead of in Canada, John might be here with me now. I wish I could expunge that thought from my mind, once and for all.

We had spent our honeymoon on Prince Edward Island, that delightfully unspoiled maritime province near Nova Scotia, where the twentieth century seemed to be slow in arriving, and when we returned fifteen years later we were pleased to find that it still had the same quiet appeal for us. Our hotel was an old one, dating back to Victorian days, and while by no means opulent by New York standards, it had an air of stability and grace so often lacking both in country inns and big-city hotels.

We chose to stay in one of the dozen or so attractive cottages that bordered the wide expanse of lawn instead of in the main building, since that way we had not only more privacy, but the luxury of our own sitting room, where we could relax and read in front of the pine-scented fire on a chilly evening. The weather left nothing to be desired during those bright midsummer weeks. The cool mornings we spent walking on the narrow country roads that meandered through fields of incredibly brilliant wildflowers, sometimes picking little baskets of the wild strawberries that grew in profusion on the sunny slopes. These we'd save to have with the tea a maid brought over to us late in the afternoon. Then, after lunch, when the sun was hottest, we'd make our way through a pine grove down to the wide sandy beach, and swim in the surprisingly warm waters of the Gulf of St. Lawrence. I think there's a current, something like the Gulf Stream, that accounts for the temperature.

Unfortunately, or rather, tragically, that last day we did not swim or walk up the beach to watch the fishermen mending their lobster pots; instead we went for a sail in the sloop that belonged to the hotel, and that was captained by the son of the owner. Besides ourselves, the only other passengers consisted of a family of four, father, mother, and two little boys, aged about six and eight. The gulf was calm, the sun was bright, and a light breeze swept us along steadily and pleasantly. We had been sailing for almost an hour, too long, I suppose, for little boys to sit still, when the younger one leaned too far over the rail and tumbled into the water.

It is difficult for me to remember the order in which things happened after that, but I do know that the mother screamed and screamed, and that the father leaned futilely over the side trying to reach the boy, who was by then several yards behind us. John acted quickly; he kicked off his shoes, dived over the side, and swam back toward the floundering child, who fortunately was wearing a life preserver, one of the old-fashioned canvas ones filled with kapok. I wasn't worried then; John was a strong swimmer, and in a few moments we could see that he had taken hold of the boy, turned him on his back, and started to tow him toward the boat.

All would have been well, too, had not the captain in his anxiety to help brought the boat about just as the wind picked up. We swung around violently—as if the boat were out of control—and raced toward the pair in the water. John had no time to swerve out of our way: I think he was trying to protect the child from being hit when the bow struck him on the side of the head and knocked him unconscious. By the time we had him back on board he was dead. The child escaped with minor injuries.

I realize now that for several weeks after the accident I did not function normally; it was enough to try just to get through the long, long, empty days. I was urged by my brothers and parents alike to spend what was left of the summer in East Hampton. So much better for you, they said, to be with people than all alone in that city apartment. Eleanor told me later that it was Dr. Bronson who advised them to let me have my way.

"He said you were the kind of person who needed to sort things out for yourself, Julia," she said. "And of course he was right."

God knows there was plenty to sort out, and plans to be made for the future. Like many others of our generation, John and I had lived up to our income and had not saved very much. During the twenties he had risen steadily in his law firm, and we both felt that a secure and comfortable future was assured. This is not to say we spent money lavishly, but we did live in an expensive and really quite lovely Park Avenue apartment, and had never seen any reason to stint ourselves until the market crashed. I suppose that in a way I was like my mother then, assuming that I would always be taken care of.

Shortly after John's death, after the funeral expenses had been paid, one of the partners in his firm, Tom Ashcroft, made my financial position clear to me. It was really quite simple; anyone could have understood it. Apart from an insurance policy on John's life, I had nothing except a few pieces of good jewelry and the furnishings of a five-room apartment. There had been a little over a thousand dollars in the checking account, but some of that had gone to pay for the funeral, and I had thoughtlessly dribbled away most of the rest before I came to my senses.

"The insurance company offers you either a lump sum, Julia," Tom Ashcoft said, "or a lifetime annuity. I strongly advise you to take the latter; in these unsettled times it would be the wiser choice, and you'll be assured of seven hundred and fifty dollars a year for as long as you live."

"But the rent on the apartment is more than that," I began.

"Yes," he said. "I know. You will have to find a less expensive place, or you'll go into debt. Could you move in with your parents? That might be one solution. I know it won't be easy, Julia, and I don't want to sound unsympathetic, but I must be realistic. John would have expected it of me."

As I rose to leave his office he stood up and came around from behind the desk to see me out. Then, pausing for a moment with his hand on the doorknob, he smiled down at me. "I wish I could be of more help," he said quietly. "Anyway, your rent is paid until the first of October. That will give you a little over a month to look around. Would you be willing to consider some sort of employment?"

I replied that I certainly would, but as I rode uptown from Forty-second Street on the Madison Avenue trolley (no taxis now), I wondered what on earth I could do that someone would pay me for doing. I wasn't even well educated; I had been "finished" at Miss Cartwright's exclusive establishment, made my debut into society, and led the life of a young socialite until I married John. Where could a thirty-five-year-old woman who had never worked in her life, who had no special skills, no training of any sort, find employment? I hadn't the faintest idea, and to tell the truth, I was rather frightened at the thought. I did wonder briefly whether I should take a course in shorthand and typing, but dismissed that thought when I looked over the few advertisements in the paper the next morning and saw how poorly secretarial positions paid. The twelve to fifteen dollars a week being offered (sometimes only ten) would not enable me to keep the apartment, nor was there any guarantee that I would find a job after completing the course. And that would mean money wasted.

As I saw it, my only salable asset was the ability to speak fluent and idiomatic French, thanks to a series of excellent French governesses and a year in Paris. But the thought of being a governess myself did not appeal; I had never had anything to do with children, and wouldn't have known how to handle them.

I drifted aimlessly through the first weeks in September, letting the others take care of moving my parents back to the city, and wishing I did not have to think of moving myself. I was toying with the idea of talking to Rick about the possibility of my living in the East Hampton house when he phoned and asked me to have dinner with him. He apologized for taking me to the Schrafft's on Seventy-ninth Street instead of to a posh restaurant, saying that things were pretty tight just then. I was fairly certain that Rick wanted something of me, but was completely unprepared for the demands he made in the course of the meal.

"You heard that Gil was let go, didn't you, Julia?" he asked when we were seated.

"Oh no, Rick! What is he doing?"

"Moving heaven and earth trying to find another job," he answered. "So far the only prospect he has is selling life insurance, and—well, you know Gil—that isn't his cup of tea."

"What about Margo's family?" I asked. "Can't they help?"

"So far they've shown no sign of it. But he's only been out of work a week, and they're still up at the farm. Perhaps they haven't been told."

"Will he be able to keep his apartment?" I asked, thinking of the lovely Fifth Avenue duplex Margo had furnished so tastefully.

"That's what I wanted to talk to you about, Julia. Gil can't go on contributing to Mother's and Father's support at present. And I can't pay the whole thing. . . ."

I had completely forgotten that I would be expected to continue the payments John had been making, and suddenly saw most of my seven hundred and fifty dollars a year disappear.

"I can't give them what little I have, Rick! What will I live on?"

"That's just it, Julia. You'll have to—"

"No!" I must have spoken louder than I intended, because several people at nearby tables turned to look at us.

"Sh!" Rick said softly. "Just listen. . . ."

It was worse than I had anticipated: Annie was to be dismissed, I was to move in with my parents and continue the fifty-dollar monthly payments, while Rick took over Gil's share.

"That means I'll have to pay a hundred a month, Julia, and that's honestly all I can manage. If I had more, Annie could stay on—"

"You mean I'm to be the maid on top of everything else?" I was aghast.

"For God's sakes, will you please tell me what else we can do? They're our parents, after all. We can't send them to the poor house."

Both of us were angry, and I think Rick was embarrassed. We remained silent while the waitress cleared the table and brought our coffee.

"I haven't told Father," Rick said after a while, "but I've had to sell the car. It's too expensive to maintain. We'll have to make some other arrangements to get them down to East Hampton next summer."

"What are you going to do with the money you got for it?" I asked. "And how much was it?"

"Only five hundred. Oh, I know that car cost over ten times that a couple of years ago, but that's all it would bring. Hardly anyone can afford to keep a car and chauffeur anymore in New York. I was lucky to get that much."

"You didn't answer my first question, Rick. What will you do with the five hundred?"

"Well," he said slowly, not raising his eyes, "I thought I'd use it for their general expenses. . . ."

I didn't want to embarrass him further, or anger him, by asking if he'd considered using it to pay his share of the rent for five months, but I thought he might have had that in mind. I waited a moment before speaking.

"You know, don't you, that five hundred dollars would cover Annie's salary for some time to come?" I asked quietly. "Or would you prefer to save it and let me be a slavey?"

"Of course not," he said shortly as a deep blush spread over his face. "I just didn't think of it, that's all."

"Then it won't be necessary for me to move in with them, will it?"

"How do I know what you'll do? You'll have to live some-place."

"I was thinking about staying in the East Hampton house for a while—"

"Julia, are you crazy? You know it's only a summer place; you'd freeze to death down there. And even if you had no rent to pay, you couldn't exist on seven fifty a year. That's only sixty-two dollars a month, two dollars a day. The best thing, and you know it, would be for you to move in with Mother and Father. Come on, let's get out of here."

We hardly spoke as he walked me back to my building, and when I was alone in the elevator I found myself wondering whether I could trust him. It was pretty obvious that he had not meant to tell me about the sale of the car; that had slipped out by mistake. And he hadn't said anything more about the hundred thousand that had disappeared. I did not like what I was thinking.

And then there was Gilbert; I felt as sorry for him as I did for myself. His adoration of Margo was such that I knew he'd work his fingers to the bone to pay for the luxuries she demanded—her clothes, her lunches at the Plaza, her dancing lessons—all of which she would expect to go on as if Gil were still a vice president in a large New York bank. She's probably the only member of the family who isn't miserable, I thought as I warmed some milk to take to bed with me. I left the saucepan to soak in the sink, forgetting that I'd be the one to clean it in the morning. I'd let my one remaining maid go weeks before, but I kept forgetting. . . .

The hot drink sometimes helped me to sleep, but that night it had no effect. I lay awake, thinking about the sorry state we were all in, and trying desperately to come up with a plan that would enable me to stay in the rooms John and I had been so happy in for fifteen years.

The next morning, however, I was forced to take a harder look at my situation. A member of the company that managed the building phoned requesting permission to show my apartment to a prospective tenant, and asked if two o'clock that afternoon would be a convenient time. I was somewhat surprised because I knew there were several vacancies on other floors, but then I realized that mine was one of the more desirable apartments, a corner one, with both southern and eastern exposures.

I think it was then that, totally wretched and close to tears, I gave up all thought of being independent and resigned myself to moving in with my mother and father. The knowledge that a number of my friends had been forced into doubling up with their parents—it was happening all over—did nothing to cheer me. I tried to tell myself that they needed me, that I could make their old age in those straitened circumstances more bearable, but that line of thought didn't help very much either.

5

Once my mind was made up, I moved quickly; I could not afford to put our furniture in storage, so I sold everything in the apartment except my clothes, my jewelry, and a few of the wedding presents. John's clothing I gave to the St. Vincent de Paul Society; I couldn't bear to sell that. When the rooms were empty I turned the keys over to the super-intendent and took a taxi up to Ninety-second Street; I couldn't manage my suitcases on the trolley.

Aside from two or three brief afternoon visits, I had spent no time with my parents since their return to the city just after Labor Day, and I suppose on those occasions I had been too wrapped up in my own affairs to give them my full attention. Once established under their roof, however, I could not help but be aware of how rapidly they were aging, and how narrow their lives had become. Most of their time was spent in the overcrowded living room, Father in the big leather armchair that had been his favorite in the library of the old house, and Mother in the upholstered rocker that had once stood at the side of the fireplace in her sitting room.

At first I could not understand why they refused to go out, even for a little walk in the park or on Fifth Avenue, but when I realized how increasingly difficult it was becoming for Mother to get around on account of the rheumatism in her knees and feet, and how unsure of himself Father seemed to be, I thought it might be just as well if they remained indoors, tiresome as that might be for them.

They were both annoyed at me for sending for Dr. Bronson when Mother stumbled over an ugly old leather hassock and hurt her wrist, but it was obvious that she was in severe pain, and I was afraid it might be broken. It turned out to be badly sprained, and after he had taped it up Dr. Bronson wrote out a prescription for a mild sedative. I saw him to the door, and was thanking him for coming so promptly when he motioned to me to step out into the elevator lobby with him.

"Your mother will be all right, Julia," he said. "It's your father who needs watching. Have you noticed any change in his behavior lately?"

"Only that he's awfully quiet; he hardly talks at all. . . ."

"Just so. He's afraid of slurring his words. The right side of his face is drawn down a bit, an indication that he's had at least one slight stroke, possibly two or three. He's an intelligent man, and he probably knows this. If what I saw in his face is the only paralysis he has sustained, he'll go on functioning until he has another stroke. Keep an eye on him; don't let him drink too much; in moderation it won't hurt him. And call me if you are worried."

I told him I would, and as I went back into the apartment I suddenly understood why Father would get up so often and disappear into the master bedroom, which was adjacent to the living room, separated from it by heavy sliding doors. He pretended he needed to use the bathroom, but I am rea-

44

sonably sure, even quite sure, that he was helping himself to a drink from his hidden supply. I was curious about the boxes Annie had told me were under his bed, but there seemed to be no way for me to examine them. With the exception of mealtimes, when the three of us were together in the dining room, Father had the bedroom under constant surveillance. The sliding doors were left open during the day, and from where he sat in the living room he had his bedroom in full view. So I had to wait.

I am afraid that I was not too conscientious about heeding Dr. Bronson's admonition that I keep a close eye on my father. Oh, I did try, but the atmosphere in those rooms was so depressing that I found myself making excuses to escape. For instance, instead of having Annie telephone for the groceries I would walk over to the Daniel Reeves store on Lexington Avenue and put in the order myself. Later in the morning a boy would wheel his delivery cart through the alley to the basement of the building, where our purchases would be loaded onto the dumbwaiter and sent up to the kitchen.

I reasoned that if I got out each day, even for a short time, I would be better company for them, and better able to endure the long hours indoors. I feel guilty about that now, but I didn't then, and as time went on I stayed out longer and longer. There was no point in going downtown to the department stores, since I had no money to spend, so when there were no errands, I would just walk. It was a pleasant enough neighborhood—not that it could compare with Seventy-first Street—but it had its good points. Joseph Duveen, the art dealer, had built an elegant two-story gallery next door to our building; I remember walking past it one Saturday morning when the large windows on the Ninety-first-Street side were wide open, affording me a glimpse of two

Gainsborough paintings, *Pinkie* and *The Blue Boy*, hanging on either side of a magnificent mantelpiece.

That block, between Madison and Fifth, was really quite good, with substantial-looking town houses (no brownstones, though) on the north side of the street, and Andrew Carnegie's palatial home (sixty-two rooms, I heard) taking up at least half of the south side. On the northeast corner of Ninety-first and Fifth, one of the Astors, I forget which one, had built a huge mansion with a curved porte cochere where occupants of chauffeur-driven cars could disembark shielded from the elements. Yes, it was rather a pleasant block, and I enjoyed walking through it.

Sometimes I'd go over to a branch of the Public Library on Ninety-sixth Street near Third Avenue, but their selection of new books was limited, and I often came away empty-handed. There was one of Womrath's lending libraries down at Eighty-fourth and Madison, where they had all the newest titles, but they charged fifteen cents a book.

On rainy days (except on Fridays, when there was an admission charge) I sometimes went to the Metropolitan Museum of Art, and it was there one afternoon in mid-November that I ran into Grace Cochrane. I hadn't known Grace at school—she didn't go to Miss Cartwright's—but during the time Ben was courting her I saw her frequently. We were never what you would call "close," but I feel sure we would have been good companions had Ben lived.

She seemed genuinely glad to see me when we met in front of Sargent's *Portrait of Madame X*, and insisted on taking me back to her spacious Fifth Avenue apartment for tea. I was afraid I'd feel awkward, but Grace was so tactful, so full of goodwill, that I was completely at ease and able to talk about the reverses our family had had without embarrassment.

Grace listened, and sympathized, but thank heavens she didn't pity me. I could not have stood that.

"So many people Ned and I used to see seem to have gone into hiding, Julia," she said seriously. "It's as if they're ashamed of having come down in the world, of having lost their money. Don't you do that—you mustn't. Besides being beautiful, and you really are, you know, you're an intelligent woman. Don't let your parents tie you down; I know only too well how easily that can happen. It would have happened to me if my sister Carrie hadn't read me a lecture. . . ."

We talked quietly, comfortably, for about an hour; when I was leaving she urged me to come again, and said she'd be in touch with me about a little dinner party she was planning.

The rain had stopped, and although it was almost dusk as I walked home, a faint afterglow remained in the sky behind the museum, and I didn't hurry. I walked slowly, thinking about my wardrobe and wondering which one of last year's dresses would be suitable, in case I did go to the dinner party. It seemed as if hardly anyone was doing any entertaining that year; it was, as Grace had said, almost as if the members of our crowd were avoiding one another. I know I made no attempt to keep in touch after one bad experience: I met Marcy Finch, an old, old friend, in Woolworth's one morning; she was buying underwear, and held a cheap, flimsy-looking slip in her hands—she who used to order everything hand-embroidered and monogrammed from Paris! She was terribly embarrassed to be caught in the five-and-ten, and when I suggested having a cup of tea together someday she burst into tears. Her husband had been out of work for more than six months, and she was almost beside herself with worry.

"I wouldn't be good company, Julia," she said, wiping her

eyes. "I don't think I could even carry on a coherent conversation. Wait until things get better; then we'll see each other."

By the time I arrived home I had decided that I *would* go to Grace's party, although I wondered briefly if it would be right to accept an invitation I could not possibly return. Annie must have heard my key in the door, for she came hurrying out of the kitchen to tell me that Mrs. Gilbert, as she called Margo, was waiting for me.

"The minute you come in, Miss Julia, that's what she said," Annie reported, looking at me anxiously.

At that moment Margo appeared at the end of the hall, her fur coat over one arm and that season's Eugénie-style hat set stylishly on her blond hair.

"Julia, I've been waiting and waiting," she began.

"Come in here, Margo," I said, taking off my own hat and coat and leading the way into my bedroom, the door to which was just to the left of the entrance to the apartment, a good distance from the living room at the other end of the hall. It was the only uncluttered room in the place; over Mother's protests I had had the janitor take out and store half the furniture she had crammed in there, so that the room, though not large, was relatively comfortable. Besides the bed, the one from my old room on Seventy-first Street, I had retained only the rug, a fairly good Aubusson, a small desk, a chest of drawers, and two medium-sized easy chairs, which I had placed on either side of the window, with a lamp table between them. Margo perched on the arm of one of these and watched me hang up my coat and put my hat away. I had a feeling she wasn't sure how to begin.

"How is Gil?" I asked. "We haven't seen him lately."

"Perfectly miserable," she answered offhandedly. "He hates selling life insurance, or trying to sell it."

48

I waited for her to continue; I thought I knew what she wanted, but I was not going to be the one to broach the subject.

"Julia," she said at last, "we need help. We can't go on like this. We're so broke—and I thought—you see, I know about that hundred thousand dollars your father withdrew, and—"

"Margo, there isn't any hundred thousand. Those ten-thousand dollar withdrawals from the bank were lost in the Stock Market crash, or in gambling or something. It doesn't matter what happened to the money; it's gone."

"But have you looked for it? He could be hiding it." Her voice was low, but tense. "And we need it so badly. It could be divided up between you and Rick and Gil, and it would tide us over for a while. I don't know how we'll pay our bills. . . ." Her voice trailed off.

"No, I haven't looked for it," I replied crossly, "because I know it does not exist. And even if it did, I doubt that Father would know what he did with it; he can't seem to remember anything for more than five minutes. Dr. Bronson says it's a combination of stroke damage and senility. I'm sure it's only a matter of time—you've seen him, Margo, you know what he's like."

"Yes," she said slowly, "he does seem vague. He asked me the same question four times, and each time I gave him the identical answer. But, Julia, suppose it *does* exist. . . ."

Eventually she left, after borrowing a dollar I could ill afford to lend her. And I hurried in to my parents, feeling guilty at having been gone so long.

6

Grace was as good as her word; two days after I had tea with her she called, inviting me to dine informally on Friday of the following week. I was hesitant about leaving my parents alone for dinner; they had become accustomed to my being at the table with them. But then, it had been such a long time since I'd had any social life at all—anyway, I decided to go. I said nothing to them immediately, but phoned Rick and persuaded him to dine with them that night. He agreed so reluctantly that I was tempted to say that the least he could do would be to give me an evening off; after all, I was bearing the whole burden of my parents' care. But I did not want to make him angry; he might have changed his mind and refused to come at all.

After I hung up I turned my mind to my wardrobe. In earlier years I would have had several dinner dresses from which to choose, new ones, too, or else I might have gone out and bought one for the occasion. Fortunately I had purchased a few dresses the previous fall, when the styles changed so drastically. The short, straight lines of the flapper days had been supplanted by longer, gracefully flaring skirts of mid-calf length, ever so much more becoming to anyone over fourteen. I selected a wine-colored silk as being the most appropriate, and carried it into the kitchen to see if I could press out a few wrinkles in the skirt.

"Sure, and an evenin' out is what you're needin', Miss Julia," Annie said with a smile when I told her about the dinner party. "You've been too cooped up with the old couple. Here, let me press that for you; you might be scorchin' it. My, that's lovely and soft, that silk is."

It was indeed soft to the touch (I've always adored pure silk), and when I put it on the night of the party the rich folds made me feel elegant for the first time in months. When I finished dressing I was satisfied with the reflection I saw in the glass; the warm tone of the fabric was right for my coloring, dark brown eyes and even darker hair that curled just enough to be manageable, which was fortunate, since I could no longer afford a hairdresser. I had applied powder and rouge sparingly; I never did like any suggestion of the "painted look," and besides, I've always had a good complexion. After putting a drop or two of perfume from my last bottle of Guerlain's L'Heure Bleue on my wrists, I was ready. And ever so glad to be going.

The evening was not only pleasant, it also turned out to be profitable to me. I knew only one of the other guests, Rob Lewiston, who owned a popular bookstore down on Fifty-ninth Street. His sister, Ellen, had been at Miss Cartwright's with me, but I had never seen very much of him; he didn't go out in society very often, in spite of the Lewiston money.

He was a fairly tall man, with light brown hair, alert gray eyes, and a pleasant smile, dressed rather casually for a dinner party, I thought. I remember wondering whether Adelaide Graham had married him for his looks or the Lewiston money; poor woman, she didn't have a chance to enjoy either for very long, having died in childbirth within a year of the wedding.

Two other couples completed the guest list; a Professor Garrett and his wife; and a French couple who were in New York on business, the legal end of which Ned Cochrane's firm was handling. Monsieur Dulais had some English, enough to get by on, but Madame had none, so that when I spoke to her in French her face lighted up and she made a great show of telling Grace how good my accent was. I was only too glad to chat with her and to translate what the others were saying from time to time, to the relief of Grace and Ned, both of whom admitted to only a rudimentary knowledge of the language. Professor Garrett, who was placed next to me at dinner, must have been impressed, because he asked me if I had ever considered teaching French.

"I am not asking out of idle curiosity, Mrs. Wilcox," he said. "Just the other day a colleague of mine asked if I knew of anyone who would be interested in a part-time teaching position—"

"Oh, I'm afraid I wouldn't qualify," I said quickly. "I've had no professional training—"

"In this case it would not be necessary," he interrupted. "Not for a private school. If you should be interested, let me know, and I'll see that you have an interview." And he handed me his card.

Rob Lewiston, who was sitting on my other side, asked me where I was living (he must have heard of John's death, but, of course, he didn't mention it), and when I told him he first looked astonished and then he burst out laughing.

"I'm sorry, Julia," he apologized when he saw my puzzled expression, "but it really is funny that I haven't seen you. People say I go around with my eyes on the ground, and

53

maybe they're right; you see, I live in the same building. What floor are you on?"

"We're on the sixth, the south apartment," I replied.

"Then I'm directly below you. I wonder why Grace didn't tell me; I could have picked you up. But then, she called me at the bookstore. Well, at least I can see you home."

I was very glad he did; I had not minded taking the Madison Avenue trolley down to Seventy-sixth Street and walking the one block over to Fifth, but when we left the Cochranes' building it was snowing, and I welcomed the warmth of the taxi the doorman hailed for us. Also, it was pleasant to have an escort at that hour of the night.

That had been on Friday, and on Sunday morning Rob phoned to ask if I would have dinner with him that night.

"I know it's short notice," he said, "and you're probably busy—"

"No, as it happens, I am not, Rob, and I should enjoy having dinner with you."

"Good. If you like German food, there's a good place over on Eighty-sixth Street."

"Do you mean Gustav's? I know it. John and I used to like their sauerbraten."

"Then you know it's not too fancy. Would six be convenient?"

This time I didn't bother to call Rick; one or the other of my brothers generally dropped in on Sunday afternoon, which broke up the day for my parents, and when I spoke to Annie about dinner, she said she'd see to everything. No one had come by six, though, when Rob called for me. In spite of that, Mother and Father seemed content enough, although apathetic is probably a better word. I felt a little guilty about leaving them again so soon, but after all, I had spent most of the day with them.

Rob wanted to take a taxi, but I said I had been in the house all day and would like a walk. Besides, I didn't really know how affluent he was. By that time I had become so accustomed to watching every penny that I guess I expected everyone else to do the same. I needn't have been concerned in Rob's case, though, for in the course of the evening I learned that his parents' estate, a fairly substantial one, had been divided equally between him and his sister, Ellen, three or four years previously.

"It's rather ironic that I should have the money now," he said toward the end of our meal. "It would have been much more helpful ten years ago when I was starting out. But my father washed his hands of me when I left law school after one year. He'd talked about my succeeding him in the firm ever since I can remember, about the clients he'd turn over to me, all that. So when I didn't 'measure up,' as he put it, I was on my own. Fortunately my mother understood that not everyone wanted to be a lawyer, and since she had money of her own she was able to lend me enough to get the bookstore started."

He paused while the waiter took our orders for dessert.

"It was a while before I could show a profit, so when Adelaide and I were married we couldn't afford anything grander than the apartment I'm in now. Then she died—"

"But why stay there, Rob? Surely now—"

"Plain laziness, Julia. It's comfortable enough, and I'm not in it that much. A woman comes in by the day to take care of the laundry and cleaning and so on. I get my own breakfast, and she leaves me some kind of meal if I'm not dining out. So why bother to move? I hate to think of packing all the books I have in there. So I stay."

Somehow Rob's easygoing, quiet manner encouraged me to talk more about myself than I would have thought possible. I did not go into the details of John's death, but I was frank about my dissatisfaction with my living arrangements.

"Recently I've begun to feel as if I have no life of my own, and I seem to be unable to do anything about it. I'm too selfish not to resent the demands my mother and father are making on me." I stopped abruptly, feeling I had said too much.

"It's not a matter of being selfish," he said quietly. "It's that you're caught in a set of circumstances over which you have no control."

"I think I'll call that Professor Garrett and see about teaching French," I said impulsively. "Maybe that would help change my point of view. And surely they could spare me for a few hours a week."

"Sounds like a good idea," he said. "And you can't tell where it might lead. I would give it a try, Julia."

On the way home in the cab he asked me if I had plenty of reading material. "I can let you have almost anything," he said. "The new Rinehart mystery, *The Door*, is pretty good. Give me a list of what you want, and if I don't have them at home I can bring them from the store."

When I mentioned Edna Ferber's *Cimarron*, which had recently been published, and a book by Hugh Walpole, he nodded.

"I could send them up on the dumbwaiter," he said with a chuckle. "If you hear the ropes rattling some evening, it won't be the butcher or the iceman, just the bookman."

"You'd probably frighten the life out of Annie," I warned. "She's nervous enough about that dumbwaiter as it is, afraid a robber might come up on it. Really, Rob, I'm serious. I've had to promise to see about having a bolt put on it so that it can be opened only from our side. So if you have any books for me, you'd better phone, and I'll run down and pick them up."

"Any robber who gets on that dumbwaiter will be taking his life in his hands; those ropes look pretty worn to me. But you're right, of course. No point in frightening the help," he said as the cab drew up in front of our building.

Annie did not look frightened when I got home, but I could see that something was troubling her, and thought at once that Mother or Father had been taken ill.

"No, no, Miss Julia," she said. "The mister and the madam were just as usual, but . . ."

"But what, Annie?"

"Mr. and Mrs Gilbert came . . ." And she hesitated again.

"Oh, I'm glad they did, Annie. Then my parents weren't alone all evening."

"Yes, Miss Julia, but it struck me sort of strange, like . . ."

Apparently Gilbert and Margo had arrived shortly after Rob called for me and said they were staying for dinner.

"And they ate everything in sight, Miss Julia. I'd made enough lamb stew for us for two days, and it's all gone. And Mrs. Gilbert kept askin' for more biscuits, more of this, more of that, and her so thin and all. It looked like they were starvin', it did. And then she was all over the place, snoopin' like. And Mr. Gilbert so quiet . . ."

7

The next morning I made two telephone calls: one to Professor Garrett, who said he'd be pleased to arrange an interview for me with the headmistress of the Martingale School; and the other to Rick. It was so unlike Gilbert and Margo to arrive unannounced and uninvited for dinner that I was concerned. I'm not sure why I thought Rick should know about their strange visit; perhaps it was because with Father in his present state, my oldest brother seemed to be the head of the family—anyway, shortly after ten o'clock I called him at his office and told him what Annie had said.

"And she claims that they ate everything in sight, Rick, as if . . ." I could not go on.

"As if they hadn't eaten for a week, you mean?" he finished for me. "I doubt it, Julia. Margo probably had him out walking all afternoon and they'd both worked up an appetite. You know how she is about exercise. But I'll ask Eleanor to have them over tonight or tomorrow and see if I can find out what's going on. Don't worry."

He rang off before I could tell him about Margo's

"snoopin'," and maybe it was just as well; it might have sounded catty on my part. All the same, I was sure that Annie knew what she was talking about, and equally sure I knew what Margo was looking for.

I think it was then, just after I'd hung up the receiver, that I began to wonder if my sister-in-law could be right—that there might be a vast sum of money hidden someplace in the apartment. And I suppose I blame Margo, in a way, for planting that seed in my mind, a seed that took a deeper root than I realized at the time, and that eventually determined the course of my life.

But more of that later . . .

On Tuesday Rick called and said that Gilbert and Margo were thinking of moving up to her parents' farm, but that they were going to hang on in New York as long as they could.

"You've met her parents, Julia, the Elkinghams. Well, it seems they've been hit pretty badly and are putting the house on Eighty-second Street on the market. They didn't even bother to open it this fall."

"You mean they might all be living on the farm?" I asked, thinking how difficult it would be for Gilbert to accept charity, and wondering what on earth he would do with himself all day.

"Maybe, maybe not," Rick answered. "If things start looking up for Gil, they won't have to."

How Margo would hate the rural life, I thought. I knew she enjoyed summer vacations in the rolling country of the Hudson Valley, with horseback riding, tennis, and swimming parties, as well as the occasional winter weekend when she and Gil would go up for the skiing and skating, but I was sure she would take a dim view of year-round country life without the house parties and elaborate entertaining.

That, however, would be *her* problem, not mine. I just hoped Gil would not become despondent; Margo would see to it one way or another that she got what she wanted, but I was afraid my handsome, badly spoiled brother would suffer.

After Rick's call I hurried out to do the errands, and knowing I'd be cooped up in the apartment all afternoon and evening, I put off my return until lunchtime. Annie would be out; she had kindly changed her afternoon and evening off from Sunday to Tuesday, so that I could have dinner with Rob. How I hated those "Sundays and every other Thursdays" when I could not leave the premises! But Annie had to have some time off—I think she spent it with cousins in the Bronx—and my parents could not be left alone. Even if they had been in good health I could not have gone out; all their lives they had been accustomed to having someone within call to fetch a book, a cup of tea, or whatever, and our reduced circumstances had not changed that.

Fortunately they both dozed a bit after lunch, Mother on the chaise in their bedroom, and Father in his big chair in the living room, so I could count on about an hour to myself. Generally I read, but that day I was restless and unable to settle down with my book. I suppose I could lay the blame for my actions on what Annie had said about Margo, but that might not be fair. In any case, after Annie had finished the lunch dishes and left and the apartment was quiet, I decided to go through all the closets and chests of drawers that were not visible from the living room.

There was a connecting door between my room and the one next to it, so I started there. I had wanted to make that room over into a sitting room for myself, but Mother insisted upon leaving it as a bedroom in case we should ever have an overnight guest. ("Whoever heard of a home without a guest room, Julia? It simply is not done.")

Like all the rooms in the apartment, mine excepted, it was overcrowded; a large double bed with intricate carving on the head- and footboards was enough by itself to dwarf the room, but Mother had added two night tables, each with a large bronze lamp on it, a bureau, a dressing table, and three occasional tables with tooled-leather tops. These last I remembered from the parlor of the old house, where they had fitted nicely, but they looked completely out of place in that room. Most offensive was the mirror, not the beautiful Venetian one, Father had that in his bathroom, but a large circular one in a heavy frame decorated with cupids and garlands, and that belonged in a ballroom, if indeed it belonged anyplace at all.

I was glad that the rooms were connected by a door that closed, instead of by an open archway.

I found nothing of interest in any of the drawers, which were filled with old cashmere sweaters, fragile chiffon scarves, and exquisite handmade French lingerie, lavishly trimmed with lace, articles Mother had saved over the years. I can't imagine why she did; with the exception of a few woolen shawls, nothing in those drawers would be useful to her in her old age, certainly not the peignoirs and nightgowns, which had obviously been made for a slim, youthful figure. Perhaps she used to take them out and look at them once in a while, and think about when she had worn them.

And that made me wonder about her marriage; looking back, I could remember that Father was always most considerate about her comfort and well-being, but did he love her? I can't be sure. When I came across a large leather-bound album of pictures taken on their honeymoon, I carried it into my own room. Without question Mother had been a beauty; the photographs show a young woman with masses of light blond hair and the delicate features of a porcelain figurine.

One of the early pictures shows her standing next to my father in front of the Trevi Fountain in Rome; he is smiling down at her, almost laughing, the epitome of the happy bridegroom, while she gazes coolly at something out of the camera's range. She should have been smiling up at him, I thought—although it is possible that she was pregnant with Rick at the time and did not feel too well.

Just then I heard the tinkle of the little silver bell Mother used to summon Annie, and went to see what she wanted. I was becoming used to being the maid on those Sundays and alternate Thursdays, and while I no longer resented the position, I can't say I ever liked it. When I went in to see what she wanted she was back in the rocking chair, and ready to give instructions about her afternoon tea.

"Good and hot, Julia," she said, "but not too strong. And the Darjeeling, please."

Annie had set the tray out before she left, so there was not much for me to do except to warm the pot, put the kettle on to boil, and measure out the tea. (The A&P's own brand, but Mother didn't seem to notice.)

I had never been taught to cook, but under Annie's tutelage I was learning to do a few things in the kitchen. Of course she made it easy for me; generally there was a casserole or a stew of some kind that needed only to be heated, and a bowl of washed salad greens waiting to be dressed. Annie didn't trust me to roast or broil, or to bake anything except potatoes, and even then she'd leave a note telling me what time to put them in the oven. And she would have made a custard or a pudding for dessert. The good woman even asked me to leave the dishes for her to wash up in the morning, but I felt the least I could do was to put the kitchen in order for her —I guess it made me feel virtuous.

That night, though, I was tired and out of sorts by the

time I had dried the last dish and put it away in the china cabinet, but it was still too early to go to bed, and I had lost interest in the book I was reading. I was standing in the doorway of the room next to mine, wondering how I could fill in the evening, when I noticed the closed door of the closet in one corner of the room, and realized I hadn't checked that. I waited until I heard my parents preparing for bed before trying the knob. The door was locked (I wondered if Margo had tried it), but the key to my own closet fitted it easily. It was really more of a dressing room than a closet, with a marble sink surmounted by a mirror on one wall, and shelves and clothes hangers on the other two. But there were no clothes there at all, just piles of boxes, all sizes and shapes, stacked one above the other, and every one of them tied with white cord.

My hands were suddenly cold, and I felt my heart begin to beat faster. My common sense told me I had not come upon the missing money; even in small denominations, a hundred thousand dollars would not have filled all those boxes. But I did have a feeling, or, more accurately, a hope, that valuables of some kind had been stored away there. I had just lifted down the topmost box, a small one, when the telephone rang, sounding shrill in the quiet apartment; it startled me, causing me to jump and almost drop the box. I put it down on the marble basin and hurried out into the hall to answer the call before the ringing disturbed my parents.

"I know it's late, Julia," Rob Lewiston said, "but I had a bunch of paperwork to catch up on at the store. I brought a couple of books home for you; I could run up with them if it's convenient."

When he came I felt dreadful about not being able to invite him in, but I could not very well entertain him in my bedroom, and as for taking him into that awful living room with Father snoring in the next room. . . .

So I thanked him at the front door as graciously as I could and made up something about just getting my parents settled for the night, which I'm sure he believed, because at that moment Father shouted from the far end of the hall wanting to know who was calling at that hour.

"Is that someone for me, Julia?" he called out.

Rob grinned as he thrust the books at me and then quickly took himself off.

I did not get back to the closet that night; by the time I had explained the late caller to Father and seen him back to his room, Annie came in, and I had to spend a few minutes telling her how the dinner went off. I suppose I could have stayed up late going through the boxes, but I decided to wait—something to look forward to, I guess.

8

The next day, Wednesday, was a better one: Annie was there, leaving me free to go out as I pleased; I had two new books to read; and Professor Garrett called to tell me that Miss Steele, the headmistress of the Martingale School, would see me at eleven o'clock. And I still had the boxes to investigate. I thought I would try to save them for another day, a long dull Sunday when Annie was out. It sounds childish, I know, for an intelligent, mature woman to act that way, but at that point my life was so humdrum that I was ready to grasp at anything that would alleviate the boredom. I knew it would be prying, that I had no business poking into those boxes, but, I rationalized, wasn't it possible that Father, or even Mother, had hidden away valuables that had been in the vault and forgotten about them? And we did need money so badly. . . .

I was pleased at the way the interview with Miss Steele went off. She was not at all concerned with my lack of teaching experience, only with the quality of my French. Her own accent was excellent, but she took the precaution of having a Madame Soulier, an elderly French instructor, on hand to double-check on mine. The older woman's schedule was too heavy for her, I was told, and someone was needed for four hours a week to relieve her of the conversation classes. The pay was minimal, a dollar an hour, and Miss Steele apologized for it, saying she knew it was low, but that perhaps the pleasant association with her girls would help compensate. And could I start the next day?

Armed with a copy of the text being used, I walked slowly home, thinking how easy it had been, and that the four dollars a week would be clear profit. In good weather I would not even have to pay any carfare, since the school was at Eighty-first Street near Park Avenue, within easy walking distance of the apartment.

I paused for a moment or two in front of a small shop to look longingly at the single dress displayed in the window, a beautifully tailored shimmering gray silk, belted at the natural waistline with a wide strip of crimson crushed velvet. Alongside the dress, tastefully arranged on a small glass-topped table, lay the accessories: a pair of gray French kid gloves, a small leather purse of the same shade, and a cloche hat that matched the belt. What I wouldn't have given to have been able to walk in and order the whole ensemble! Instead I went home to lunch and informed my parents of my employment.

I was sure Father would disapprove, since he had always held the working woman in low esteem. I didn't think Mother would care one way or the other. It was she, however, who was aghast at my doing what she called "menial labor" (I guess washing up her dinner dishes was something else), while Father merely grunted and went on eating his floating-island pudding. When my mother rose at the end of the meal she stood for a moment holding on to the back of the chair to steady herself, and looked at me more severely than I ever remember her doing.

"Please keep this to yourself, Julia," she said sternly. "I would not have it known among my friends that you are disgracing the family."

With that she turned and hobbled slowly away from the table. I was tempted to hurl a sharp retort at her retreating back, but when I saw how pathetic she looked, leaning heavily on her silver-headed cane, all I felt was pity. It is possible, I thought, that she can't help feeling as she does. In her day, in the society in which she moved, it *was* considered a disgrace for women to work.

As Miss Steele had hoped, I found the association with "her girls" quite pleasant. If the class had been composed of young children I doubt that I would have enjoyed it; these students, however, were well-dressed, well-mannered girls in their mid-teens, who, if not exactly anxious to become proficient in French, at least gave the appearance of trying to please. The work itself did not tax me; most of the time I followed along the lines suggested in the text, but on occasion I would invent a word game, or set them to playing simple charades in French. The hour passed quickly; in fact, during the time between Thanksgiving and Christmas, whole days seemed to slip away from me. I began to see more of Rob Lewiston, for one thing, and while no serious relationship developed between us, I found him an affable companion for an occasional movie or dinner, or even just a Sunday-morning walk in the park. We talked easily about the past, my years with John, his with Adelaide, but he never pressed me for details about my life with my parents; after my little outburst in the restaurant the first time we had dinner together he must have realized what the situation was, but he never brought it up.

I liked him for that. I also liked the way he kissed me lightly when he said good night to me at my door.

During that time I hardly heard from my brothers. Of course I knew that neither one of them was having an easy time of it, but still it annoyed me that they called so infrequently, shrugging off all responsibility for our parents. It was as if they were saying, "Julia's taking care of things, so why bother?" Eleanor was the only one who came on a regular basis, and it was she who kept me informed of the troubles of the rest of the family. Rick, she said, was making her economize drastically in all areas.

"At least you have Annie, Julia," she remarked just before leaving one afternoon. "I have only a woman to clean once a week. We've taken the girls out of Miss Cartwright's and put them in the public school, and thank goodness they seem to like it. And Rick has been talking about moving to a less expensive apartment; poor thing, he's working so hard, and looks so worried. And he's tired, so tired; I think we're all tired these days."

Gilbert, she said, was doing better; he had managed to sell a few policies and annuities to some of his more fortunate old friends, ones who had not suffered as we did in the crash.

"I think it took Gil a while, Julia, to swallow his pride and approach men he'd known socially. I heard him say that it made him feel like a beggar, but I guess he thought that would be better than living off Margo's parents."

I said that it wouldn't hurt him to come to see his own parents once in a while, and then apologized for sounding waspish.

"I know how you feel, Julia," Eleanor said soothingly. "It doesn't seem fair that you should have it all on your shoulders. It *isn't* fair, and I am constantly amazed at your patience. You're really very good to them, you know, even though they don't seem to appreciate it. I wish I could help you in some way—other than visiting once in a while. But it won't go on forever, you know that."

After she left I stood at the window of my room staring disconsolately at the roofs of the houses across the avenue, thinking about Eleanor's last remark. Suppose my parents were both to die in their sleep tonight, how would I feel? Sad? Relieved? Probably both. But then what? Where would I go? How would I live on sixty-two dollars a month—no, more like seventy-eight now that I was earning four dollars a week. Even so, I'd have to move into a rented room in a boardinghouse, like Lily Bart at the end of *The House of Mirth*. Whether they lived or died, the future looked anything but rosy.

The day after Eleanor's visit was one of Annie's Thursdays off, and since she would be off the coming Sunday as well, I was feeling more than a bit gloomy. I'll get back to those boxes, I thought as I walked home from the French class. After Annie leaves, I told myself, right after lunch—no, better wait until after dinner. And if I find anything valuable, I'll sell it and keep the money. If I'm to be the maid for two days a week, shouldn't I be paid for it? And who would ever know?

I felt a tingle of excitement in my spine as I let myself into the apartment, and knew then that I would not be able to wait until evening to satisfy my curiosity. After Annie leaves, I said to myself, I'll just take out one box, bring it into my room, and be ready to push it under the bed if anyone interrupts me.

Lunch was endless that day, and Annie seemed to take longer than usual to clean up. I'm not sure why I thought I had to wait for her to leave; she always knocked, even when

71

my door was open. I guess I was just nervous, or maybe slightly ashamed. When at last she left, after reminding me to heat the oven before putting the chicken pie in to cook, I went quickly to the dressing room, picked up the box I had left on the marble basin, relocked the door, and went back to my own room. It took me a few minutes to untie the white cord—for some reason I did not want to cut it—but even so, I sat for a moment before lifting the cover. I suppose I was steeling myself against disappointment.

My heart leapt when I saw the familiar robin's-egg blue of a Tiffany box inside the outer carton, just the right size and shape to hold a piece of jewelry—a diamond ring, a pair of ruby earrings, a pin set with sapphires; Tiffany's could be counted on for the best quality in gems, the very best, I knew.

I had, of course, heard the phrase "tears of rage," but until I opened that small blue box and saw that it contained only my mother's engraved calling cards, I had never experienced them. They filled my eyes, but did not fall as I threw the little box across the room and watched the elegant pieces of white cardboard spill out on the rug. How long I sat there, holding one hand over my mouth to keep from crying out, I do not know, nor do I know what distressed me more, the disappointment in the contents of the box or the sudden anger that welled up in me. I generally have more control over my emotions.

I wonder, now, what I would have done had there been diamonds or rubies there; at the time my desire for a life free of monetary worries was so strong that it never occurred to me that selling jewels that were not mine would be tantamount to stealing. I would have been a thief, but I suppose I would have avoided thinking about that. I would have rationalized, convinced myself that I was only being sensible. Would I have shared any profits with my brothers? God alone knows, and anyway, the question is moot.

I stayed up late that night, long after Annie came in and the apartment was quiet. I sat on the floor of the dressing room, hurriedly going through the rest of the boxes, not bothering to tie them up again. There was nothing I judged to be of value in any of them. Mother had saved the most ridiculous things: a pair of brocaded evening slippers with rhinestones on the heels; white kid gloves in various lengths; handbags of different colors and sizes, almost all from Mark Cross; and several boxes of expensive notepaper engraved with the address of the Seventy-first Street house. Of silver and gold there was none, but I did put aside (as a possible source of income) a pair of mother-of-pearl opera glasses and a rather lovely petit-point evening bag from Vienna. It was carefully wrapped in tissue paper, and looked as if it had never been used.

All in all, the contents of those boxes, no more than useless mementos of an era forever gone, seemed to me then so pathetic that I was close to tears for the second time, and before going to bed I rewrapped the opera glasses and the evening bag and put them back on the shelf. I did not become a thief that night. Nor did I sleep well, even though I had been up so late, and as a consequence felt miserable the next day. The French class did not meet on Fridays, and it was raining so hard that it would have been foolish to go out for a walk. As if that weren't enough, Father was in an especially trying mood, finding fault with everything from the temperature of his coffee at breakfast to the way his napkin was folded at dinner, and when he pushed his plate away with half his meal uneaten I was near the end of my patience. Nor did it end there; up until bedtime I could hear him muttering to himself in a way that convinced me he'd been drinking heavily all evening.

When at last he was quiet I threw myself into a chair in my room, exhausted, wondering how many more days like that I would be able to endure. I hadn't felt so wretched and alone since John's death the previous summer, and was about to go to bed in tears when I noticed one of Rob's books on the night table. A moment later I had slipped out of our apartment and was ringing the bell of the one below.

"Julia, how good to—" Rob stopped speaking when he saw the tears that sprang into my eyes, and after drawing me into his hallway and closing the door he folded me into his arms. A few moments later he led me over to an old leather sofa in the room directly beneath mine, which he had made into a study of sorts, with bookshelves covering every inch of wall space.

He kept one arm around me while he handed me his handkerchief, a lovely Irish linen one, with an "L" embroidered in one corner. He didn't speak for a while, and I was content to be quiet and lean against him with my head on his shoulder. Later on, when I was completely calm, it seemed the most natural thing in the world for us to become lovers.

In the morning, to Annie's astonishment, the boy from the Greek florist on the corner appeared with a dozen long-stemmed roses for me. I arranged them in one of Mother's cut-glass vases and kept them in my room.

9

As Christmas approached and the city, in spite of the depression, began to take on a holiday atmosphere, I knew I should make some preparations to lighten the gloom that hung over our family, but whatever I thought of doing simply cost too much. A tree, for instance, was out of the question; even if I could have spared the money for one, I couldn't imagine where in that crowded living room I could set it up. And of course there would be no presents. It crossed my mind that it might be best to ignore Christmas completely, and treat December 25 as just another day to be gotten through, avoiding all references to Christmases past when expense was never a question.

There were certain things, though, that I could not help remembering: the huge tree in the drawing room of the old house, hung with scores of little hand-carved ornaments; the dozens of pots of poinsettias that lined the entrance hall; the holly and greens that decorated the mantelpieces; and the large silver punch bowl, surrounded by twenty-four matching cups, that stood on the refectory table—another world, and impossibly far away.

I saw remnants of that world, however, at the Martingale School; about ten days before Christmas a lovely tree was set up in the front hall, ropes of greenery were laced through the banister of the wide staircase, and smaller decorations appeared in the classrooms. The French conversation class was lively that week; my students needed no urging to chatter away about their Christmas lists, the holiday parties they would attend, the plays they would see, and so on. All *en français*, of course.

I was surprised and touched when on the last day of school so many of them brought me small gifts, all beautifully wrapped and marked "Joyeux Noël." After all, they didn't know me very well—I'd been there such a short time—and I said as much to the headmistress when I was leaving.

"They can well afford to be generous, Mrs. Wilcox," she said with a smile. "And besides, I happen to know you rate highly with them. And we're all very glad to have you with us."

I was inordinately pleased to know that I was making a success of my little job; maybe it was because so few people had said anything complimentary to me lately—I don't know. Anyway, as I carried my bag of presents up Madison Avenue, I felt happier and more light-hearted than I had for a long time. I would be able to give some presents after all, I thought. Surely among those packages there would be bath powder, handkerchiefs, or cologne, the sorts of things Mother used to buy for me to give the teachers at Miss Cartwright's. I would at least have something for Eleanor and Margo and Annie—and Mother, of course.

Any elation I felt, however, was short-lived. As soon as I entered the apartment I heard Father's angry voice and then Gilbert's quieter one coming from the living room. As I hurried down the long dark hall, past a white-faced Annie standing in the kitchen doorway twisting her apron, I realized that my father had lost complete control of himself.

"No, damn it, no, no, no! I will not lend you any money!" he shouted at Gilbert. "You sniveling, groveling—you're nothing but a good-for-nothing beggar! I've a mind to—"

He stopped for a moment when he saw me, but only for a moment. Then, as Gilbert turned to reach for his overcoat on the chair behind him, Father leaned over and, looking like a wild man, wrenched Mother's cane from her hand. Margo, who had retreated to a corner of the room, screamed and covered her face with her hands. Father started to raise the cane as if to strike Gilbert, but when it was no more than waist-high, he faltered.

"I—I—I—" That's all I heard clearly; after that he made a series of incomprehensible sounds—not words, but sounds like words coming out all wrong. Then he fell heavily onto the carpet and lay still, with his head up against the ugly leather hassock.

Dr. Bronson later told me that, shocking and violent as Father's death was, it probably spared him the ignominy of spending his last years in an institution of some sort.

10

Reactions to Father's death were varied: Rick worried about burial costs, Gilbert worried about being the cause of the fatal stroke, Mother wondered which of her black silks to wear, and Margo wanted to know if there was a will. As for me, I tried to force myself to think of Father as he had been when I was young, to obliterate the picture of him as he'd been this last year.

As far as I know, Annie was the only one who shed a few tears for him. And it was Annie who called my attention to the change that came over Mother in the days that followed Father's interment in the Hastings family vault. I suppose I had expected my mother to withdraw from us all and nurse her grief, or else go into a gentle decline. I had read of that happening when a spouse died after many years of marriage. But she surprised me; instead of retiring into herself, she hobbled about the apartment, giving orders for this or that piece of furniture to be moved, checking the contents of the silver chest, and making out menus, once more playing the role of mistress of the household.

The most unexpected development, and one for which I am at a loss to give an explanation, was the change in her attitude toward me. Her manner was kinder, gentler, and she made an effort to show her appreciation of any little thing I did for her. She even asked about the French class, a request I found remarkable in view of her earlier disapproval of my employment. Such an about-face! To this day I do not understand it, unless she thought her original reaction was what Father would have expected of her.

"You said you had one of the Caldwell girls in your class, Julia," she remarked one afternoon when we were having a cup of tea. "She must be the granddaughter of Emily Caldwell; you remember the family—they had that showplace in Southampton. Tell me, who else is in that school that I might know?"

I don't mean to say she turned into a saint overnight; she was still demanding and haughty, even waspish at times, but perhaps that was when her rheumatism was bothering her. It wasn't too long after Father's death, probably only a week had elapsed, when she turned her attention to her own room and asked Annie to remove all the boxes from under Father's bed. I had been anxious to do just that, but hadn't known how to make the suggestion, and when I volunteered to help, Mother nodded.

"Yes, do help Annie, Julia," she said. "And move my chair over there where I can see better. I want to know where he put my jewels."

"Your jewels, Mother? I thought they were in your drawer. . . ."

"Don't look so surprised, my girl. Haven't you noticed that I've been wearing nothing but this same string of pearls ever since we moved here?"

"Mother, why—"

"Because he insisted the rest would be safer packed away; I wouldn't be so apt to mislay them, he said. As if I would do such a thing! And he would brook no disagreement. Now I want them."

"But they are *your* jewels, Mother," I said quietly. "Why did you let him—"

"If you think I could stop him from doing exactly what he wanted to do," she replied grimly, "I don't think much of your powers of observation. Now go on, help Annie. Some of those boxes will be heavy, because that's where he kept his whiskey, too."

They *were* heavy, and it took Annie and me both to lift them out. Most of the bottles were empty, and in the end we found only half a dozen unopened ones, one of which I secreted to take downstairs to Rob. I don't think Mother saw me put it aside; she was too interested in finding her jewels, and kept getting in our way as she tried to peer under the bed.

"There!" she exclaimed suddenly, pointing to a suitcase that had been hidden behind the last of the cartons. "That's where he will have put them. Open it, Julia! Quickly!"

She was almost in a frenzy of excitement by the time we found the key—it was in one of the pockets of the suit Father had been wearing when he died—and lifted the cover. The Cartier, Tiffany, and Gorham boxes were all there, along with the colorful little lacquer jewel case that had been on Mother's dressing table in the old house—every last one of them empty.

"It was dreadful, Rob," I said that night as we sat sampling the Scotch, "perfectly dreadful to watch her face change. She'd been so excited, looking almost girlishly happy one minute; and then in the next all the life went out of her, and she turned into a crumpled old woman. She didn't cry; it might have been easier for me if she had, because then I could have tried to comfort her. She just said, 'Well, he had his way right to the end,' and went into the living room and sat with her back to us."

"You think he did sell them?" Rob asked. "Could he have pawned them?"

"Who can say? I've looked everywhere, gone through everything. There's no pawn ticket, no bill of sale, nothing."

"Strange, isn't it," he said thoughtfully, "to think your father was driven to such lengths. He must have despised himself. And even stranger to realize the control he had over your mother. Was she afraid of him? Did she ever rebel?"

"Not that I know of," I answered. "But then, until the market fell apart, she had everything she could ever have desired. Unless—" I paused, remembering her expression in the picture taken at the Trevi fountain.

"Unless what, darling?"

"I was just wondering what kind of marriage it really was; there was a picture. . . ." and I described the one I had come across.

"What you're saying, then, is that there may never have been any real love between them, is that it? That it was all a front?"

"Possibly," I replied. "She was beautiful, and he was handsome; they made a stunning couple, and there was all that wealth. For years the society pages were full of news about their doings, their travels, the dinners they gave, you know. Pitiful, isn't it?"

"If it *was* all on the surface, yes, but then I don't believe you'll ever be sure that they weren't in love at some point," he answered as he put down his glass and reached for me. "And speaking of love, my darling Julia, will you stay here tonight?"

I did stay, willingly, until the eastern sky began to lighten. I'm sure my mother never knew where I was spending some of my nights, and if Annie did, she kept the knowledge to herself.

The rest of the winter went by uneventfully, although we were worse off financially than ever, since Father's annuity payments stopped with his death. Only fifty dollars a month was involved, which doesn't sound like much now, but without it we had to economize on every blessed thing. Fortunately, food was relatively inexpensive then, and, too, Annie was not an extravagant cook; she knew how to make the cheaper cuts of meat palatable, and since Mother and I had modest appetites, a minimum amount of food sufficed.

Naturally, no money was available for new clothes, and that irked me dreadfully. I had always preferred a fine wardrobe to expensive jewelry, and up until the time of John's death I had been able to buy almost anything I fancied. I suppose that is what made it so difficult for me to become reconciled to "making do" with what I had. Small of me, I know, not admirable at all to be fussing about clothes when the papers were full of hardship stories about starving families, suicides, and all, but some habits die hard. I did try, though; the striking navy blue suit I saw in a shop window as I walked down Madison Avenue to school might just as well have been on the moon, so far was it beyond my reach. I would have loved it, but I knew better than to spend even a minute yearning for it. I knew also that I would have minded our poverty more, much more, if it hadn't been for Rob; the hours we spent together after Mother was in bed made up for a lot, and probably saved my sanity. Eventually we talked of marriage, or rather, Rob mentioned it fairly frequently, urging me to consider it.

"I'm well enough off now, dearest, to provide for you and

for your mother," he said one night as I prepared to go upstairs. "There should be no problem locating a companion for her so that you'd be free. And we wouldn't have to stay here; just find me an apartment with room for thousands of books, and you can furnish it any way you choose."

It was tempting, very tempting, but I needed time to think; would Mother feel deserted by everyone if I moved out, even if she were well cared for? And had I known Rob long enough to be sure I loved him? I didn't say that to him, though; I merely said that I'd like to wait until fall, since by that time John would have been dead for over a year.

"Yes, I know it sounds crazy," I said when I saw his smile. "Here I am having an illicit affair with the man downstairs, and having no qualms about that, but still feeling concern about the proper period of mourning."

"Just don't stop coming downstairs, darling, and I'll manage to hold out until the fall," he said, pulling me close to him and kissing me. "Now you'd better beat it, before I drag you back into the bedroom."

As I said, the rest of the winter was, except for my love affair, unremarkable, and it wasn't until late March that anything noteworthy occurred.

"Do you know what day this is, Julia?" Mother asked one evening as we were finishing dinner.

"Of course. It's the twenty-first of March, the vernal equinox," I replied, and then seeing her glance at me sharply, I realized what she meant.

"Oh, Mother, I forgot! It's your anniversary—"

"It matters not, Julia," she said quietly. "Forty-seven years, think of it! Forty-seven long years."

"I remember the big party on your fortieth—" I began.

"All show," she interrupted as she folded her napkin and

slipped it into the heavy silver ring. "All show. That's all it ever was." With that she pushed herself up from the high-backed armchair, grasped her cane, and went slowly from the room, her lacy shawl, which had slipped down from one shoulder, trailing behind her. I watched her, thinking how suddenly and how completely the energy she had displayed immediately after Father's death had disappeared the moment she saw the empty jewelry boxes. Would he have been redeemed in her eyes if the diamonds and sapphires had been there? Perhaps that was what she wanted, the knowledge that he had not taken back the gems he had showered on her over the years.

11

As the spring advanced and the days became warmer, I began to think about arrangements for the summer. Mother would expect to go to East Hampton as usual, I knew, and she would probably want me to be with her. She and Annie and I could manage there as well as we did in the apartment, although I would certainly miss Rob's company. I had not discussed the matter with my mother, and it's probably just as well, because suddenly the matter was taken out of my hands.

I had just carried the tea tray into the living room that rainy Sunday afternoon toward the end of April when Rick and Eleanor arrived with the news that they had decided to leave New York and move into the East Hampton house permanently.

"Rick will open his own law office in the village, Julia," Eleanor explained. "There's a quaint little building there that's just the right size, and we'll—"

"You see," my brother interrupted, "it's only a matter of time before my firm folds; it's losing money by the hour, and I don't want to wait until the last bell. Better that I leave now and get started on my own."

"But how will you manage in the winter? You said yourself, Rick . . ." I began.

"Yes, I know, Julia," he said hurriedly. "But it's feasible; we'll have the summer to make the place habitable for the winter—plenty of time. All it will involve will be a heating system, weather stripping—storm windows can wait—and a few other changes. No tremendous expense; labor is cheap down there."

"When do you expect to move?" Mother asked. "And what about us, Julia and me? Will we go with you?"

"Of course you will come with us, Mother," he answered, looking at Eleanor, who nodded affirmatively. "Our lease is up at the end of May—we may leave before then—and since this apartment is on a month-to-month basis, there won't be any problem about vacating it."

I suddenly understood what he had in mind, and his next words confirmed my thought.

"You see, Julia, I can't afford to go on paying two-thirds of the rent here while I'm setting up in business out on the island." He took me aside at that point and spoke quietly so that Mother wouldn't hear him. "As you know, the house comes to all three of us on Mother's death, but I would like the use of it for the time being. We'll take care of her, and naturally you are welcome to stay with us until you get on your feet."

Of course he didn't want me; that was obvious. But then, neither did I relish the thought of living in a household in which he was the master. I almost said as much then and there, but I didn't have a chance. Rick went on talking about the arrangements he was making, how a friend of his would pick Mother up and drive her down, and so on. I only half-listened; I felt completely left out, unwanted, as if I were just in the way. I believe Eleanor sensed that, because she kept looking at me anxiously from time to time. I wanted to reassure her, tell her that I would be all right, but that was not the moment. Poor woman, she'd have enough on her hands with Mother there. . . .

"And of course Annie must go as soon as Mother leaves," Rick was saying. "You certainly won't need her anymore, Julia. But look, I'll pay my share of the rent here through June; that will give you time to sort things out, close the place up. Just see that Mother doesn't bring too much stuff with her, will you? And let me know what your plans are."

At that Eleanor looked so distressed that I almost told her then that I intended to marry Rob Lewiston in the near future, but Rick would have heard me, and I was mean enough to think that it wouldn't do any harm for him to worry about me a little. I was too badly hurt to be charitable.

Three weeks later I was alone in the apartment. When Mother left for East Hampton in mid-May, she seemed to be under the impression that I would be following her soon,. and I don't think she realized that this was not the regular summer exodus, that the move was for good. It seemed kinder not to disillusion her. A tearful Annie had packed her suitcase and gone to live with her cousins in the Bronx, and suddenly, in spite of the surplus of furniture and furnishings, the apartment seemed empty.

It wasn't so bad at first, it was even quite pleasant; I could come and go as I pleased, and of course I had Rob. He was genuinely delighted when I told him I no longer wanted to wait until the fall to marry him, and started to make plans immediately.

"I certainly don't approve of the way Rick handled things,

darling," he said, holding me close to him, "but at least some good came of it: you're to be mine that much sooner. I just wish we had time to get a license and all before I go off on this trip. . . ."

Unfortunately there was a bookseller's convention or a book fair, I forget which, on the West Coast, and he felt he had to be there.

"If only I didn't have to go—but I'm committed, and it's too late to back out now. Besides, it's rather important to me. You'll be all right on your own for ten days, won't you?"

I assured him that I would be fine, that I had more than enough to keep me busy, what with the French class and the disposal of the furniture in the apartment above us.

"The days won't be long enough," I told him, "for all the things I have to do. And when you come back I'll have everything in order, so that we can get on with our lives."

The days did pass quickly enough, but the evenings were long, and I came to dread the nights; then time hung heavily on my hands, and the apartment seemed to be alive with strange noises I had never noticed in the past. I tried to convince myself that there was no reason in the world for me to be nervous, to act like a child afraid of the dark, but that didn't do much good. Before going to bed I checked the lock on the window in the dining room, the one that gave on the fire escape, and lowered the shade. The other thing that worried me was the dumbwaiter door, and I berated myself for not listening to Annie and having a bolt put on it. The janitor could have done it, but he would have expected me to pay him, and I had so little money that it never did get fixed. I made myself look into the kitchen before going to bed— what good that did I can't imagine—but I didn't actually go in there; I was afraid I might see a mouse or something worse.

So, after making sure the front door was securely bolted, I locked myself in my own room and tried to read myself to sleep. Sometimes this took until two or three o'clock in the morning, with the result that I slept late the next day.

Rob had left on Monday, and about eleven o'clock in the morning of the following Friday (what a long week it had been!) I finished my breakfast of tea and toast, and turned out my purse on the dining-room table. I had only a few dollars, but I wasn't worried, since I expected to have some money later in the day from the sale of some of the furnishings. Pride, I suppose, had kept me from disclosing my financial status to Rob, and anyway, I knew that I could manage one way or another until we were married. Then everything would be different.

I had just started to make a list of the pieces in the dining room to be sold when the phone rang. A man with a deep, rather pleasant voice, who identified himself as Seth Barnes, said he would like to see me. At first I thought he was one of the furniture dealers with whom I'd been in touch, but that was not the case.

"I knew your father, Mrs. Wilcox, long ago, but I've been away—"

"My father died last December, Mr. Barnes—"

"Yes, I know," he said. "I saw the notice in the papers. I'm sorry I couldn't get here in time for the funeral, but I was out of town. I'd like to call on you this evening to express my sympathy. I'll be there at eight o'clock." And before I could protest, the line went dead; I couldn't tell whether we were cut off or whether he'd hung up.

I couldn't remember anyone named Barnes, but Father must have had hundreds of friends and acquaintances in the business world whom I had never met; at his funeral service I had recognized only a handful of his former associates among the crowd. I thought briefly of calling Gilbert to see if he knew who Mr. Barnes might be, but I wasn't sure where to reach him, and let it go. If only Rob had been there . . .

I do not think I would have been at all uneasy if it had not been for the abrupt termination of the telephone call. He hadn't even asked me if eight o'clock would be a convenient time for me. I thought I might simply ignore the ringing of the doorbell, but then decided that company of any kind might be a pleasant alternative to a lonely evening spent listening for strange noises. And he had sounded like a gentleman.

Shortly before eight o'clock I brewed some coffee, poured it into the heavy silver pot to keep it warm, and carried a tray into the living room. As I sat awaiting his arrival, I spent the time making more lists of articles I wanted removed. I amused myself by picturing an attractive, even a charming room, free of clutter, with the two good little love seats on either side of the fireplace, three of the smaller armchairs arranged for easy conversation, the library table against the wall with the Tiffany lamp at one end, and a few other lamps on small tables in the right places. The rocker, the big leather chair, the hassock, and other odds and ends would have to go. I had just made a mental note to be sure to save the Tiffany lamp when the doorbell rang, announcing my visitor.

"Mrs. Wilcox," he said gravely, extending his hand, "I can't tell you how sorry I was to hear of your father's death. He did me a good turn once. A fine man, a fine, upstanding man."

I knew at a glance that Mr. Barnes had not been a business associate of Father's; he lacked the smooth facade that characterized so many of the ones I had met. And he was much younger than my father, mid-forties, I would say. If it hadn't been for his eyes being a little too closely set, I might have thought him handsome in a rugged sort of way. He stood about six feet, and had the look of one who had been an athlete in his youth. His hair and eyes were dark, the nose aquiline, and the mouth rather thin-lipped. No, not handsome, but definitely attractive, especially when he smiled. Any misgivings I had had about him quickly disappeared.

"Do you travel a great deal, Mr. Barnes?" I asked when we were settled in the living room. "You said you'd been away."

"Yes, I've had business that's kept me abroad. And you, Mrs. Wilcox, are you a traveler?"

While we chatted about places in Europe we'd both seen, I noticed that his eyes seldom left my face, almost as if he were studying me; it was flattering, but I began to feel a bit self-conscious. When we had exhausted the subject of travel, a silence that threatened to become embarrassing caused me to offer him some refreshment.

"Would you care for some coffee, Mr. Barnes? I have some ready."

"No, yes—that is . . . Look, Mrs. Wilcox, I'll be frank with you: I really did come to offer my condolences, but there's another reason, which I dislike mentioning, but I feel that I must. I hope you won't take offense—"

"I don't understand—"

"Your father owed me money, a lot of money, a hundred thousand dollars, to be exact." He watched me closely as he spoke.

"Mr. Barnes, my father died penniless—"

"I don't see how that can be, Mrs. Wilcox," he said, shaking his head. "He may have had nothing of his own, but he was holding that money for me until I got back—"

"Got back? From where?"

"From abroad. I was in Africa for several years." He was

speaking quietly, almost gently. "Your father didn't tell you about our agreement?"

"What on earth are you talking about?"

"He didn't tell you where the money came from?"

"He never mentioned it," I said. "I don't understand this at all."

Mr. Barnes sighed, and then leaned forward in his chair, fastening his eyes on mine.

"Perhaps I'd better explain," he said in the tone of one who is about to tell a story to a child. "You know there's Prohibition, yes? Well, years ago I ran a big operation, dozens of bootleggers worked for me, and your father was one of my customers, a good customer. Many a time I delivered liquor to your place in East Hampton. He brought me a lot of business. Always paid promptly, and paid well, because of the risk involved. Of course I was the one taking the risks, big ones. At first I went out at night myself to the foreign ships beyond the limit to get the liquor and bring it in. That was rough work, even in good weather, and you couldn't count on its staying good once you left the shore.

"Then I got a break; my boss had an accident, and I took over the distributing end. No more bad nights in a small boat. Well, to make a long story short, I struck it rich—there was plenty of money to be made in bootlegging—but something told me it wouldn't last. And it didn't; one of my men was picked up by the Coast Guard and they got him to talk. But before that happened I'd asked your father about investing some money for me. He said he'd be glad to do it provided he got three percent of the profits. So when I first had word of trouble brewing—no need to go into that now—I gave him a hundred thousand in cash. I knew I could trust him, and he came through. When I phoned him and said the mob was after me, had put a tail on me, and that I was afraid I wouldn't make it to his office, he arranged to have the money picked up. And I managed to get out of the country alive. I stayed away for eight years, until the government wiped out the last of that mob. And now I'm back."

He paused, and held out his cup for more coffee before speaking again.

"What do you think he did with it, Mrs. Wilcox? Where did he put it for safekeeping?"

12

It took me even longer than usual to get to sleep that night. Mr. Barnes had stayed quite late, asking questions about Father's affairs, his will, what had been in Mother's name, and so on. With it all he was extremely considerate, apologizing for being so persistent, and although I rather liked him I had a feeling that here was a man who had better not be antagonized. That's why, I suppose, I thought it wiser to leave him with the impression that I had never heard of the hundred thousand dollars or the ten-thousand-dollar withdrawals that had so puzzled Rick. Nothing, however, would shake my visitor's conviction that the money was safely hidden away, waiting for him.

"It must be safe, Mrs. Wilcox," he said as he at last prepared to leave. "Mr. Hastings would not have gambled with it or lost it. He was a man to be trusted. He would never have deceived me. Perhaps I should talk to your brothers; they might be able to give me a lead."

"Why did you come to me first?" I asked.

"This was given as your father's address," he replied. "It seemed the logical place to start."

"I'm afraid my brothers will be of no more use to you than I've been—"

"I'll just have to try," he said with a rueful smile. "It's important that I know what happened to it. But I mustn't keep you up any longer."

As I said, I did not sleep well that night; I kept seeing Seth Barnes's earnest face, the dark eyes bent on mine, and hearing his voice insisting that my father was an honorable man. Apparently he'd been fond of Father, and unless I misread the signs, he liked what he saw of me. I thought he held my hand a second or two longer than necessary when he said good night, but I may have imagined that.

Saturday and Sunday passed slowly, without incident; if Seth Barnes approached Rick or Gilbert, they said nothing about it to me. My brothers would, I felt sure, deny any knowledge of the missing funds in order to protect Father's good name, which, I suppose, was what I had unconsciously been doing under Barnes's questioning.

To help pass the time that weekend, I busied myself with little things, putting my clothes in order, buying what food I needed (mostly canned things that I could just heat up), and taking long walks in the park in the hope that the exercise would help me sleep better. It didn't seem to do much good.

On Monday morning, however, something good did happen: when I returned from teaching my class shortly before noon, I found Annie sitting in the lobby of the building, with her suitcase at her feet and a large black-and-white cat on her lap. I don't know when I've been so glad to see a person.

Half an hour later her clothes were back in her closet, the cat was shut up in the kitchen with a bowl of milk, and Annie and I were sharing a can of Campbell's tomato soup in the dining room. She had seemed so distraught that I insisted she wait until after lunch to tell me what happened.

"You can't know how terrible things were, Miss Julia," she said, putting down her spoon. "My cousin, name of Bridget, is at her wits' end, she is. Mike, that's her husband, has gone and lost his job. He's willin' enough to work, but he couldn't satisfy the boss. He says there's a right way and a wrong way to nail up coffins, and Mike somehow couldn't get it right. So he gets sent off, and feels so bad that he stops at a speakeasy on the way, and has no money at all when he gets home.

"And next day they had no rent money—they owed back rent, too—and got put out of the flat and had to go to Mike's brother's, where there's six children in three rooms. And such rooms, Miss Julia! On the ground floor and damp, and no heat except what comes out of the stove. Dirt everywhere, and varmints! I'll be washin' every stitch of my clothes, even though I didn't unpack there. And one toilet for four families; I never saw the like of it. Poor Bridget's cryin' her eyes out; their own flat was a palace compared to that."

"The cat, Annie," I said when she paused to wipe her own eyes. "Where did he come from?"

"Such a nice cat, Miss Julia. Name of Patrick, seein' as how they found him a year ago St. Patrick's Day. Poor thing, what with the children tormentin' him, and Mike's brother kickin' him when he was in drink, and nothin' for him to eat. I couldn't leave him, so I brought him. He'll be no bother, and he'll keep the mice out."

She sighed as she folded her napkin, then she took a deep breath and looked at me.

"I wouldn't want you to think they put me out, Miss Julia. They'd never do that, but I couldn't see any place to sleep, unless it was on the floor—and all that filth! Oh, Miss Julia, if I could just stay here . . ."

Of course she stayed, and took immediate charge of the housekeeping again, insisting that the roof over her head and

99

a clean bed at night would do instead of wages. I guess she knew I hadn't been doing much cooking, because she said if I could spare fifty cents, she would make us a good, tasty Irish stew for dinner.

Later that afternoon when I told Annie that Rob and I were to be married, she looked so distressed that I was puzzled; I had thought she'd be delighted.

"What is it, Annie?" I asked. "Don't you like Mr. Lewiston?"

"Oh, no, Miss Julia. It's not that—it's just—well, I guess you won't be needin' me—"

She was so close to tears that I put my arm around her shoulders and assured her that not only would we need her in our new quarters but that we'd be able to pay her wages. Poor soul, she must have had visions of returning to the Bronx.

"Miss Julia," she said slowly after blowing her nose and putting her handkerchief away, "even if we're movin' out of here soon, I'd best give this place a cleanin'. 'Tis more'n a bit dusty. Will we be takin' the pictures and things with us?"

"I'm going to sell most of the furniture, Annie, but we'll keep a few things; the silver tea set, of course, and those two Dutch paintings. They were always favorites of mine."

"But not the one of the old gentleman?" she asked with a hint of a twinkle in her eyes.

I glanced up at the portrait of my father's father, a forbidding-looking old fellow with muttonchop whiskers. Ben used to say Father kept him hung over the mantelpiece in the library of the old house to scare away burglars.

"We'll sell him if we can, Annie," I replied. "We might get a dollar or two for the frame. I'm sure neither Rick nor Gilbert would want him." No, I thought to myself, it isn't likely that they would. In fact, they had shown no interest in any of the furnishings, not even the silver. Of course they had both been well fitted out with all those kinds of things when they married, but it did surprise me a bit that neither one of them had asked for any of the few valuable pieces that were left, the Audubon tea set, for instance. They both needed money, and they could have sold that. But then they'd have had to explain its disappearance to Mother.

While Annie bustled about with her brooms and mops, I went from room to room listing the articles I would keep instead of those to be sold. Since I wanted only a few things—the Dutch pictures I mentioned, the silver, the Tiffany lamp, the Venetian mirror, and two of the better end tables, it seemed simpler to do it that way. I had intended to attach tags to these articles, so that the dealer would know they were not for sale, but Annie called me for the Irish stew before I got around to it. Perhaps, in view of what happened at the end of the week, it was just as well.

13

I slept soundly on Monday night—Annie's presence across the hall from me made all the difference—and felt sure of another good sleep on Tuesday. I do not think I even took a book to bed with me; no, I'm sure I didn't. I simply opened the window slightly, turned out the light, and slipped in between the smooth, clean linen sheets Annie had put on the bed that morning. I half woke up sometime during the night, thinking I heard someone moving about in the hall, but just then a trolley car went past on Madison Avenue, and the noise of it drowned out all other sounds. When it had gone by I listened for a moment, but heard nothing.

Probably just Annie taking the cat off her bed and putting him in the kitchen, I thought, and turned over.

The next morning she told me the dumbwaiter door had been partly open when she went into the kitchen, and asked again if I would have a lock put on it.

"It's so loose, Miss Julia," she said. "Any little draft blows the door open, and then mice or anything can get in."

"Well, we won't be here much longer, Annie, but as soon

as Mr. Lewiston returns I'll get him to fix it," I said, and was about to ask her if she had been up in the night when I thought better of it; if she hadn't, the combination of the open dumbwaiter door and my thinking I'd heard someone in the hall might have been enough to send her back to her cousin Bridget—anyway, I didn't want to upset her.

The next few days were busy ones for me; I saw various used-furniture dealers, and managed to empty out the room next to mine completely. One dealer made me an offer for everything in it, including the monstrous mirror with the cupids on it as well as all the boxes in the closet. Of course he gave me only thirty-five dollars for the lot, which was far less than even the little leather-covered tables were worth, but he convinced me I could not do any better, so I let it all go. Overriding Annie's protests, I gave her fifteen dollars. I think she spent some of it on food, though, because we had a couple of expensive meals: steaks and chops instead of stews. Then on Friday morning Rob called from Grand Central, saying he had to go directly to the bookstore, but would I meet him for dinner that night?

"You go right along, Miss Julia," Annie said when I asked her if she would mind being alone in the apartment. "I'll have Patrick for company, and we'll both be early to bed, and nothin' ever wakes me up till mornin' once I'm off to sleep. Now you just enjoy yourself."

I was surprised at how delighted I was that Rob had called me the moment his train got in; his eagerness to see me had been reflected in his voice, and I think it was then that I realized how much it meant to me to be loved and desired again. I felt incredibly happy as I went through the day, and it must have shown, for twice Annie asked me why I was smiling.

Over dinner Rob told me about the highlights of his trip,

and I filled him in on what had happened during his absence. He listened quietly while I spoke of the arrangements I was making for closing the apartment, and chuckled when I described Annie's return with the cat, but when I mentioned the visit I'd had from Seth Barnes he looked at me with some concern.

"Barnes?" he asked. "Are you sure, Julia?"

"What do you mean, am I sure?"

"Sure of the name, Barnes. It sounds familiar; yes, you said he'd been a bootlegger, so it must be the same one. A tall fellow with a lot of black hair? It must be the Barnes I knew—I didn't really know him, but I knew who he was. My father used to get his liquor from him, too. So did a lot of his friends. Barnes did well for himself, must have made a hell of a lot of money, but he disappeared suddenly. No one knew why. My God, Julia, and you let him into the apartment when you were alone there?"

"Rob, he seemed very nice, and he said he knew Father—"

"I know, darling, but I wouldn't have anything more to do with him if I were you. All that rot about giving your father a hundred thousand—"

"But you see, Rob, he *may* have; what he said could be true. I'm inclined to believe him, but *he* wouldn't believe me when I said there was no trace of any hundred thousand. I didn't tell him I had heard that there was such a sum, that it couldn't be accounted for, because I'm positive Father lost it gambling or on Wall Street when he was trying to salvage something, and I certainly wouldn't want that to get around—it could hurt Gil or Rick. I know that must be the case, but I couldn't say so to Mr. Barnes, so I just listened to him repeat that Father was honorable and trustworthy, and that the funds were put away safely, waiting for him."

"Of course you're right, Julia; we wouldn't want any suspicion of embezzlement to be laid at your father's door. Put it all out of your mind, darling, and let's go back to my place and see if there's any of that Haig and Haig left."

And I *was* able to put Seth Barnes out of my mind once we were settled in Rob's study, sipping our drinks and talking about the future.

"First things first," Rob said. "We'll get married next week, and you and Annie can move down here, or I'll move upstairs, and then we'll look around for another place to live. But right now I have something else in mind."

And it was while I lay contentedly in his arms, while Annie slept soundly upstairs, that someone quietly and systematically ransacked the front rooms of the apartment above us.

14

I couldn't believe my eyes when I saw the damage that had been done during the night; the dining room, living room, and master bedroom were in such a mess that I was almost afraid Annie would leave again for the Bronx, filth or no filth. She didn't though; in fact, she remained remarkably calm while Rob called the police and got the janitor up from the cellar. She didn't even give me an "I told you so" look when it became apparent that the intruder had hauled himself up on the dumbwaiter and stepped into her kitchen.

"It musta been about two o'clock when I heard the crash," the janitor said to the police lieutenant. "The rope musta broke when the guy was makin' his escape, and he musta been down around the first floor when it snapped, else he woulda been killed when the cage fell."

"You didn't get a look at him?" the lieutenant asked.

"No look at all. I got outta bed quick—thought it was the boiler—and after I checked that, I noticed the door to the alley was open, and then I saw the broken dumbwaiter, and by that time the guy was long gone."

"An unusual but not unheard-of means of entry," the policeman said. "I would have thought he'd have come down from the roof on the fire escape, and in through that window—"

"Mebbe he tried that," the janitor interrupted, "and couldn't get the fire door to the roof open. It's got a special lock at night."

"Perhaps he wasn't a pro, then." The lieutenant looked thoughtful. "Maybe some out-of-work fellow looking for money or jewels."

"Whoever he was," Rob said, "he must have been a lightweight to fit in that dumbwaiter."

"Yeah," the janitor agreed, "with anyone heavy that rope woulda broke on his way up. Wonder what he was after."

We were quiet for a moment or two, waiting for the lieutenant to tell what the next steps were.

"As I see it," he said thoughtfully, "he came off the dumbwaiter, through that swinging door, and into the dining room. He probably had a flashlight, because he wouldn't have turned on any lights until he closed the door leading to the hall."

"That's what first alarmed Annie, Lieutenant," I said. "We never close that door, or the one from the living room to the hall, and they were both shut this morning. Also the door to the master bedroom—"

"Can you see if anything's missing in here, ma'am?" the lieutenant said, turning to me.

I couldn't at first; the ornate Audubon tea set, one of Tiffany's most famous designs, was still on the heavy sterling-silver tray on the side table, and the three-tiered chest that held the flatware had been opened, but its contents seemed to be undisturbed. The table linens had been pulled out of the sideboard drawers and lay scattered about on the floor, and the leather backs and seats of the dining-room chairs had been slashed.

"Looks as if he was looking for something special, something that had been hidden away, gems, maybe," the lieutenant said. "And he must have been pretty quiet about it. A cat burglar can rob you blind without making a sound—and you'll notice that he didn't throw anything around that would have made a noise." He paused for a moment, and then turned to Rob. "You said you live in the apartment below, sir, and you heard nothing?"

"That's right," Rob answered. "But I sleep at the other end of the hall. And Julia—Mrs. Wilcox—and Annie have their rooms down at that end as well."

"And neither the fires nor the floods would wake me up once I'm asleep," Annie said.

"And you, Mrs. Wilcox, are you a sound sleeper, too?"

"Not ordinarily," I replied slowly. "But last night Mr. Lewiston and I were out late, and I was so tired when I got to bed that I don't think I even turned over until Annie called me this morning. I really slept well."

I had indeed slept well, in Rob's bed for most of the night, and by the time I slipped into my own room, the door of which, as I have said, was just to the left of the entrance to the apartment, day was dawning, and the thief was well gone.

The lieutenant nodded, and we were about to move into the living room when Annie, who had been counting the knives, forks, and spoons and replacing them in the silver chest, suddenly cried out.

"The gold spoons, Miss Julia! Every one of them gone!"

"There were twelve of them," I said in answer to the lieutenant's questioning look. "Small demitasse spoons. The thief may have thought they were fourteen-carat gold, but actually they were very good gold plate."

"And small enough to fit easily in his pocket," the lieutenant said. "That tea set over there would have been awkward, too big for him to manage. No, everything points to him being after money or jewels. What about in here? Any small objects missing from this room?"

"I don't think so," I answered, looking around at the ruined furniture. Not a cushion nor an upholstered chair remained intact, and the pictures on the walls had been taken down and had their backings ripped off. Books had been removed from the shelves next to the fireplace and piled helter-skelter on the floor, but I could not see that anything was missing.

"Whose room is this?" the policeman asked, pointing to my parents' bedroom.

"Nobody has used it since my mother left here a few weeks ago; those are her things thrown all over the beds and a few of my father's. He died last December."

The beds were torn apart, and all the drawers of the bureau and dressing table had been emptied out onto the mattresses. The door to the bathroom stood open, and we could see that towels had been pulled out of the small linen closet, but nothing in there had been smashed or broken. In the large walk-in closet next to the bathroom, coats, suits, and dresses were heaped in the middle of the floor, along with shoes, hats, purses, and whatever else had been on the shelves.

"Yep. He was looking for jewelry all right," the lieutenant repeated. "Was there—"

"No, Lieutenant," I said. "My mother's jewelry had been sold, and the few pieces I have are in my own room."

"Well, as I said, Mrs. Wilcox, he was after small, valuable stuff, probably thought there were some diamonds or other stones hidden away. There's been a spate of jewel robberies all over the city. Seems as if people are driven to theft—you know the story—they're unemployed, no money, no food for the kids, people who've never committed a crime in their lives. You'll probably never see your gold spoons again, but we'll do what we can. I'll send the fingerprint boys over, but chances are the fellow wore gloves and it'll be a lost cause." (He was right; the only fingerprints they found were Annie's and mine.)

After he left, Rob and I sat at the kitchen table drinking coffee and trying to decide what to do next. I must have looked tired, because he urged me to get some rest instead of starting to restore some semblance of order to the front rooms.

"You'll have to move downstairs tonight, Julia, you and Annie, if you're to get any sleep at all," he said, reaching across the table and putting his hand over mine. "I'll leave the key with you, and you can have her make up the beds. The maid's room is empty, she can have that, and you can—"

"Yes, I know where you want me to sleep. Don't worry. I'll arrange it so that everybody has the right bed. Are you going now?"

"Yes, I'll have to get down to the bookstore, but first I'll put a bolt on the dumbwaiter door. He's not likely to come back, but you'll feel safer, and I'll feel better about you."

What a difference there was between Rob's concern for my well-being and that of my brothers! When I phoned them later on that morning to tell them about the break-in, Gilbert said it was a damn shame, and Rick advised me to move as soon as possible.

I suppose we should have told the lieutenant about Barnes's visit and the money he was looking for, but we didn't. Now, as I look back, I can see that it wouldn't have made any difference in the end. At dinner that night, a comfortable meal in Rob's dining room, with Annie in charge of his kitchen, we decided that there were three possibilities. It could have been the ex-bootlegger searching for his money, although I did not think he looked as if he could take on the role of a sneak thief; or it might have been someone he sent to search the place, with instructions to make it look like a robbery. That would account for the theft of the gold spoons. Or, the lieutenant could be right in thinking it was a gem thief.

"Let's not dwell on it, darling," Rob said when we had finished eating the roast chicken dinner Annie had served us. "You've had enough for one day. Have you brought down everything you need for the night?"

"Yes, and I've been thinking of things that must be done: on Monday I'll have to find someone to cart away all that ruined furniture—"

"And on Tuesday we'll get married," he interrupted.

"On Wednesday I'll look for an apartment; I'll love doing that, but Rob—I might not have enough money to put down a deposit—" I broke off, too embarrassed to let him know how little I had.

"Why on earth didn't you tell me sooner, Julia?" he asked when I had explained my financial situation. "All these months you've been scrimping—I had no idea—you should have asked me—"

"No, I couldn't, Rob. Not until now."

"I'll open an account for you the first thing Monday morning; in the meantime, here, take this." And he pressed some bills into my hand.

"Sunday is a day of rest," Rob said at breakfast the next day, "but that doesn't necessarily mean it should be spent sitting around the house."

"Indeed not," I agreed. "There's far too much to be done upstairs—"

"No, not that either. Wait until you get rid of all the stuff you don't want, and you can't do that until tomorrow. Today is to be given over to pleasure. What would you like to do?"

"A walk in the park?" I suggested. "It's a beautiful morning."

"Good. We'll start with that. Then lunch at Longchamps, and after that we might take in a movie. But it's still early; would you like to look at the paper before we go?" he asked, handing me the rotogravure section of the *Times* and picking up the Book Review.

Later on, when I went upstairs to get my coat, I could hear the phone ringing as I unlocked the door.

"Julia, I've been worried sick about you!" Eleanor's voice was filled with concern. "I haven't been able to reach you—where have you been? Rick told me about the burglary; are you all right? Wouldn't you like to pack up and come down here to us? It's your home, too, you know."

"Thank you, Eleanor. You're a dear. But really I'm fine. Rob Lewiston is taking charge of things, and by the way, he and I are going to be married—"

"Oh, Julia! I'm so glad. I hated to think of you alone; I wanted Rick to go up to be with you, but he said he couldn't. Now you won't need him, not with Rob there. I'm sure you'll be happy, Julia; he's such a nice person. Bring him out here sometime this summer, will you?"

We talked on for a while, and as we did so I got the impression that the East Hampton venture showed signs of working out satisfactorily; Rick's business was slowly building up, Mother was content (they had decided not to mention the burglary to her), the children loved living in the country, and so on.

"Look, Eleanor," I said after a while, "we'd better hang up. This is an expensive long-distance call—"

"Wait a minute, Julia," she broke in. "I nearly forgot something, a piece of really good news for a change: Gilbert and Margo are moving to California! He has what looks like a splendid job with the Bank of America in San Francisco. Someone he knew at Harvard has an uncle who is a senior vice president there, and pulled some strings. Or have you heard all about it?"

"No, I hadn't heard," I replied. "But that's not so surprising. I haven't seen anything of Gil and Margo since they gave up hope of finding that hundred thousand. I am delighted, though; I was so afraid Gil would despair. I was even worried that Margo might leave him—"

"Well," Eleanor said slowly, "like the rest of us, they've been having a hard time. But I don't think you'll have to worry about them any longer, Julia." And there's no chance that they'll ever worry about me, I thought ruefully.

Central Park was sparkling that morning; the flowering shrubs along the bridle paths glowed in the spring sun, the leaves on trees that lined the walks were still young enough to look shiny and new, and every so often a faint fragrance of lilac drifted past us. Little girls, dressed in their new spring coats and straw hats with streamers down the back, pushed doll carriages or rolled their hoops, while little boys steered tricycles around them with much ringing of bells. Fat babies surveyed the scene from their handsome prams or strollers, and uniformed nurses stood guard over all. No sign of hard times here, I thought, on a path almost within sight of the abject poverty of the homeless men living on scraps in shanties in the abandoned reservoir, a pathetic little community known as Hoover Valley: despair and hopelessness so closely juxtaposed to happiness and security, all under the same benign sky.

We didn't hurry, nor did we talk very much as we made our way south on the path that ran behind the museum, past the obelisk, content to be together.

"You're very quiet, darling," Rob said as we left the inner walk and headed for the Sixty-fifth Street exit to Fifth Avenue. "You're not worried, are you?"

"On the contrary," I replied, "I'm counting my blessings. Oh, Rob, what would I have done without you? Suppose you'd remarried—"

"I guess I was too lazy to look around, too set in my ways. And besides, I never met anyone I wanted to marry until you fell into my arms. Come on, here comes a bus; do you want to sit up on top?"

Over a leisurely and absolutely delicious lunch at Longchamps we discussed the kind of apartment I should look for during the coming week.

"If I find a good two-bedroom one—"

"With a study, or, better still, a library," he reminded me.

"Yes, I know. A library, and then one of the bedrooms could double as a study and guest room, should we ever need it. And a maid's room for Annie."

"A fresh start, darling. And speaking of that, we'd better make a start if we're to see a movie this afternoon. How about *Grand Hotel*? Greta Garbo and the two Barrymores are in it, and Mordaunt Hall gave it a good review in the *Times*."

It *was* a good movie; Garbo was perfect. In fact, the whole day was perfect, but when I remember it now I have to think how unfair it was of the gods to permit me such a lovely glimpse of a future free of loneliness and poverty, only to snatch it away.

★　★　★

On Monday morning a car went out of control (it was said the driver had a heart attack) at the intersection of Fifty-ninth Street and Lexington Avenue, killing two pedestrians, one of them Robert Lewiston. He had been on his way to the bank to open an account for me.

We'd had so little time together. . . .

15

A fortnight after poor Rob's tragic death, Annie and I found ourselves living on Third Avenue near Eighty-fourth Street in two rooms, half of what was called a railroad flat. Circumstances forced me to make a quick decision about where we were to go, and as I saw it, I had two choices: either to move myself and Annie down to the East Hampton house, or to find cheap rooms for us in the city.

In the end I decided on the latter; the prospect of being in constant and close contact with a brother who didn't want me, even in a large, fairly comfortable house, and more or less under his supervision, was less appealing than independence in more modest quarters. I knew Eleanor would do everything she could to make me welcome, but even so . . .

I took Annie with me when I checked out some of the rooming houses I had seen advertised, hoping I could find one I could afford in a good neighborhood. The respectable, well-kept ones proved to be far beyond my means, and the others—well, the less said about them, the better. We were walking through Eighty-third Street when I remembered

Eleanor saying that she had looked at some cheap apartments between Lexington and Third avenues before the decision to move to East Hampton was made. We saw several that would have done nicely, but none for less than fifty dollars a month. That, I figured, would leave me exactly twelve dollars out of my sixty-two to live on. And since school had closed for the summer, I no longer had the extra four dollars a week —not that that would have helped much.

The sympathetic superintendent of the last building we tried suggested that we look farther east, on Third Avenue itself, instead of on a side street.

"If you don't mind the noise of the El, miss," he said, "you're sure to find something there."

And we did. In a building that had seen better days, we found that we could have what used to be the parlor in a four-room flat, plus a small bedroom, for fifteen dollars a month. I'd better explain: on both sides of Third Avenue, builders had erected four-story structures intended to house eight families, two to a floor. The original flats consisted of a parlor on the Avenue side, a kitchen in the rear overlooking desolate backyards, and two dark, windowless bedrooms in between. The single bathroom on each floor, containing only a toilet surmounted by a wooden water tank, was shared by the two families, and could be entered only from either of the kitchens.

By the time we moved in, the owner had divided the flats in half, so that four families had to share that meager facility. The kitchen doors were sealed up, the bathroom was enlarged slightly to make room for a galvanized tub, and the new entrance to it was from the hall. (Annie found out all this from one of the older tenants shortly after we moved in.) Enough hot water for a shallow bath was obtained by inserting a nickel in a gas-operated heater that worked erratically, and that was not often used. It cost Annie and me ten cents each to take a bath, because we felt we had to scrub out the tub before using it. Judging from the dark ring four inches from the bottom, which no amount of scrubbing would entirely remove, other tenants were not so particular. Bathing took second place to eating. I remember a Mrs. Murphy, who lived across the hall from us, putting all four of her young redheaded children into the tub at one time.

"They'll get no prize for cleanliness," she said to me with a laugh as she wrapped the smallest child in a towel, "but it's fifteen cents more I'll have for food for them."

That was after we'd been there for a while.

The fifty dollars Rob had given me paid for the van, a small one, because we didn't need to take much of the old furniture with us; there wasn't enough room for it. I thought the price was exorbitant for such a small load, but I was too exhausted to bargain or try to find another mover. The secondhand furniture dealer had worn me out; he refused to take away the damaged furniture (I had to pay the janitor to do that), and he gave me so little for the rest that I was almost in tears. He was angry, too, that I would not sell the tea set, but I knew he'd offer only a pittance for it, and besides, I wanted to hold on to it and the flatware as long as possible. At the last minute I decided to keep the Venetian mirror, although the dealer seemed interested. After all, we would need a mirror of some sort.

Annie was worried that Patrick would run away or get lost during all the commotion, and put him in the laundry hamper for safekeeping until the door of the flat closed on the last of the moving men. Once released, the big cat made a complete tour of the two rooms, meowing from time to time to let us know he did not think much of his new surroundings.

I can't say I blamed him; I didn't think much of them either.

Our windows were almost on a level with the tracks of the elevated line, and vibrated every time a train went by, shaking dust onto the sills. I slept, or tried to sleep, in the front room, while Annie took the small bedroom behind it. I hoped we wouldn't still be there when the cold weather came, since the gas logs in the little fireplace were the only source of heat. The only running water we had was in a sink in Annie's room, which also contained a two-burner stove. Altogether it was awful, perfectly awful, and we were no sooner in it than I began to scheme to get out of it.

I did not dare let myself dwell on how horrible it was, or on how far down the social ladder I had fallen, nor could I allow myself to think about Rob and the life I came so close to having with him. I would have gone to pieces had I done so. I knew it was necessary for me to keep busy, so two days after we moved I began to look for a full-time job. The employment agencies gave me no encouragement; if I did make my way to the head of one of the long lines of waiting applicants, it was only to be told that nothing was available. I don't know why they didn't put up a sign outside saying NO JOBS TODAY. It seemed as if there weren't any to be had in the entire city, just hundreds and hundreds of weary people looking for work.

Years later I read a poignant article in a magazine about unemployed men who left their families regularly every morning, ostensibly to look for work, but who had long since given up on the agencies, and instead of tramping from one to the other spent their days on park benches or in the public library, returning home empty-handed at six in the evening. Pride, I guess, kept them from letting their wives know the truth.

And it was pride that held me back from calling any of my old friends and asking for an introduction or some kind of help. The ones who might have done something for me were probably in Bar Harbor or Newport or some other summer resort, anyway. But when I came across an advertisement for a store-wide sale at Altman's, that old and prestigious Fifth Avenue store, I remembered Harry Bigelow, a onetime friend of Ben's and a frequent visitor at the Seventy-first Street house. I knew he had been with Altman's then, in some kind of executive capacity, but I had no way of knowing if he was still there. I hoped he was; I had a feeling he would give me a job for Ben's sake, if for no other reason, and I decided to try to see him.

I dressed carefully that morning; I did not want to look glamorous, as if I didn't need the job, but I knew that appearance counted for a great deal. I settled on a simple dark blue two-piece dress I had bought to travel to Canada in with John (how long ago that seemed!) and took the trolley down to Thirty-fourth Street. Harry Bigelow *was* there, and he did hire me.

"You're in luck, Julia," he said after we had exchanged greetings and I told him how much I needed employment. "We're doing practically none of the usual hiring right now, but with the vacation schedule in full swing, we can use a few relief salespeople. Take this note to Mrs. Little in Personnel; she'll set you up."

It was as easy as that: at least getting the job was easy; the work was not. No, I'm wrong; the work was not difficult, but it was tiring, and not what one would call stimulating. The hours were long and passed incredibly slowly, especially on days when there weren't many customers, which was most of the time. People simply did not have the money to spend. And I did get tired of standing; it was against the rules for salespeople to sit down, even when there was nothing to do; we had to move about and give the appearance of being

121

busy—the great store had an image to maintain, depression or no depression.

I was unaccustomed to being on my feet all day, and by the time I dragged myself home in the evening I was worn out. But I earned fifteen dollars a week, and that helped keep us housed and fed. I don't think I could have managed without Annie; she kept the little flat clean, no easy task, since dust and dirt seemed to pour into the place through the open windows, even through the cracks in the floor. She took care of my clothes, washing and ironing one of my two dark cottons each day (Altman's insisted that we wear only black, brown, or navy); she prepared my meals, and saw that I put my feet up the moment I arrived home. We had brought what remained of Father's Scotch with us, and when Annie saw how tired I was after my first day's work, she insisted I take some before dinner. After that she had a drink ready for me every night.

"Sure, an' it will do you good, Miss Julia," she'd say. "An' you after slavin' away in that store all day."

As I drank it, feeling the strength return to my body, she would entertain me with stories about the other tenants: how the husband in the family in back of us came in drunk and shouted at his wife; how the oldest Murphy boy had fallen down the stairs and cried and cried, not because he was hurt badly but because his toy car had been broken in the fall; and how Mrs. Dolan on the floor above us screamed every time she saw a mouse in her rooms.

"She borrowed Patrick for a few hours, Miss Julia, and when I went to get him she wanted to know was I yer mother. 'Twas none of her business, but I thought it best not to tell her I was yer maid, so I said you were my niece. You don't mind, do ye?"

"Of course not, Annie," I said warmly. "It was exactly

the right thing to say. And you're not my maid, Annie; you're my friend."

She shook her head at that, but I could see from her embarrassed smile that she was pleased. She earned a few dollars now and then cleaning the floors and tables in the ice-cream parlor on the corner, and the good woman tried to turn them over to me. Of course I refused to take them, but I think she simply added them to the money I gave her for our food. We did eat rather well that summer, even though we had no icebox and she had to shop every day.

July was hot enough, but nothing like August, when the baking heat that set in broke all records. The temperature in the airless flat must have been almost a hundred at times, and between the noise of the trains so close to our open windows and the heat, sleep was almost impossible. Some evenings when I wasn't too tired, we'd walk over to the East River to try to cool off, but most of the time I did not feel up to it.

I would arise in the morning unrefreshed, dreading the hours of standing around in the store, pretending to enjoy folding handkerchiefs and scarves or straightening out piles of books, depending on which department they assigned me to that day. I could see absolutely no future for me in that famous New York department store, a thought that was reinforced when a saleslady told me she'd been working there for twenty-five years, and proudly showed me a pin the management had given her to commemorate the occasion. She was still a saleslady, and never would be anything else. What surprised me was that she seemed content.

By the middle of August I was beginning to think I should have gone to East Hampton after all. And I came close to a decision to make the move as I lay in bed one steamy night, thinking of the cool breezes from the ocean, of walking barefoot on the beach at the edge of the water, of sitting in the shade of the huge maple tree on one side of the wide lawn. The images were tantalizing, and I'm fairly sure I would have succumbed to the temptation they presented if the Venetian mirror had not fallen from the wall that night with a terrible crash.

16

Glory be to God!" Annie cried out as she came running from her room. "Is it burglars after the tea set? Are ye hurt, Miss Julia?"

I managed to turn on the light in time to prevent her from stepping on the broken glass that lay scattered all over the floor, and she sighed with relief when she saw what had happened.

"I never should have hung the mirror between the windows," I said. "They always rattle when a train goes by, and the vibration must have caused it to fall. Probably the hook wasn't in firmly. Don't try to clean it up now, Annie. To-morrow will be Sunday, and I'll be here to help you. Go back to bed, go on."

When I awoke the next morning, the first thing I saw was the gilt frame leaning crazily against the leg of the small drop-leaf table we used for our meals. Pieces of glass adhered to the edges and the corners, but the frame itself did not appear to be damaged. I wondered if it was worth salvaging, and being careful to put on my slippers first, I tiptoed across the shards of glass that sparkled in the morning sun. I was about to pick up the frame when Annie bustled in with dustpan and broom and ordered me out of the way.

"You'll be cuttin' yourself, Miss Julia," she warned, "and then where'll we be? Don't we have trouble enough without that? Sure and you've heard how a broken mirror means bad luck? Stand back, now, and you too, Patrick, and I'll have this to rights in no time."

By the time I had bathed (how I hated that galvanized tub!) and dressed, she not only had order restored, but had set out coffee, toast, and soft-boiled eggs for our breakfast.

"I see no more pieces of glass," she said, sitting down opposite me, "but don't go walkin' around in your bare feet, in case I missed one. Will you be wantin' the frame, Miss Julia? There's somethin' stuck in the back of it, some papers or other."

I think I knew before I examined them what the "papers" were, and I was right. They consisted of ten bonds, bearer bonds, each for ten thousand dollars, dated 1924, and due to mature in ten years' time, two years from the time I found them. They had been pressed flat and secreted between the mirror and its thin wooden backing. For a few moments I was too stunned to marshal my thoughts, but as I sat there with the bonds in my hands, several things became clear to me: I suddenly understood the look on Father's face as he stared at the mirror that night in the old house; I understood why he kept the mirror in his bathroom, when there was a perfectly good one over the sink; and I knew why he was so anxious to know who was at the door the night Rob came up with the books. He must have been expecting to hear from Seth Barnes, knowing that at some time the ex-bootlegger would come to claim his property. What I could not understand was why he had never clipped the coupons and used the interest. Possibly he was saving it for an emergency, or maybe after his series of small strokes he simply forgot about it.

I was about to fold the bonds and put them into my purse for safekeeping when I noticed a small piece of what we used to call onion-skin paper folded in half and attached to one of them with a paper clip. When I read the message my father had left there I knew I had no alternative but to get in touch with my brothers at once.

17

I went down to East Hampton the next day, taking a delighted Annie with me. I told her only that important business had come up in connection with the papers found in the mirror, and that Rick, as a lawyer, would have to take charge of it. She nodded approvingly, and said that that was fine, but even finer was the fact that I would not be "slavin' " in that big store all day long.

Rick had been insistent that I bring the bonds out to him at once, insistent and excited, almost jubilant.

"Come immediately, Julia," he said when I phoned him from the drugstore on the next block, "and I'll call Gil. Then, as soon as he gets here, we'll divide it up. Boy, what a difference this is going to make!"

I probably should have mentioned the note when I telephoned to him, but at the time I thought it wiser to let him see it for himself.

"Wait until after dinner, Julia," he said as he drove us up from the station, "when Mother's in bed you and Eleanor and I can talk. Gil and Margo can't get here until Friday—

it's a long train ride from California—but in the meantime we can start to sort things out."

"How is Mother, Rick?" I asked, thinking how good it was that she'd escaped from the dreadful heat of the city.

"Pretty well, I guess," he answered. "You'll find her frailer, I think, and awfully quiet. Absentminded at times, too, but she seems contented enough."

She did look frail, and thinner than she had been, but her face lighted up when she saw me, and she greeted Annie like an old friend. Eleanor was as warm and charming as ever, making me think I'd be welcome even if I hadn't come bearing wealth.

"You're to have your old room, Julia," she said with a smile as she led the way upstairs. "It's pretty much as it always was, so you'll feel right at home. Come down when you're ready; I must check on dinner."

"Let Annie help you, Eleanor," I said as she started down again. "She won't know what to do with herself otherwise."

"I overheard your mother asking her to make a custard for her," Eleanor said with a laugh, "so she's probably in the kitchen already. I've put her in one of the maids' rooms off the pantry. . . ."

It wasn't until almost nine o'clock, when the children were in bed and Mother had retired to her room, that the three of us sat down at the far end of the big living room. I handed Rick the brown envelope containing the bonds and watched him count them. When he came to the last one, the one to which the note was attached, he frowned and looked across at me with a puzzled expression.

"I can't make sense out of this," he said almost angrily. "Who is this person?"

"Let me see, dear," Eleanor said, reaching for the note.

" 'These bonds,' " she read, " 'belong to Mr. Seth Barnes,

who gave to me one hundred thousand dollars in cash to hold in safekeeping for him. I first put the money into a numbered account in a Swiss bank, then, since neither Mr. Barnes nor I wanted it traced, I withdrew it, ten thousand at a time, transferred it to my own account, and put it into bearer bonds. My verbal agreement with Mr. Barnes was that I was to be allowed to keep three percent interest on the capital. I shall claim that interest when I see fit.'

"Signed 'Richard Gilbert Hastings, October 4, 1924.' What does it mean, Rick?" Eleanor asked, handing the paper back to him.

"It means," I said before he could reply, "that the hundred thousand belongs to Seth Barnes, and that the interest alone comes to us."

"To date, that would be about twenty-four thousand in accumulated interest," Rick said gloomily. "Eight thousand for each of us, instead of thirty-three plus interest. Who the hell is this Barnes, anyway?"

"Didn't he call you, Rick? He said he would—"

"That must have been who it was—someone called, I forget what he said his name was—and asked me if I knew anything about a sum of money Father was holding. I thought it was some banker, and said absolutely not, and that was the end of it. Did you say you talked to him, Julia?" Rick leaned forward and stared at me.

"Yes, or rather he talked to me—at length," I replied. "Here's what happened. . . ." And I described Mr. Barnes's visit and as much of the conversation as I could recall.

"Now I remember the name," Rick said when I paused. "His father was a fisherman, used to bring the lobsters and crabs, and the son—must have been about my age—delivered the liquor. That's why neither he nor Father wanted the money traced; it was from bootlegging."

For a while we were silent, then Rick put the bonds, together with the note, back in the brown envelope and stood up.

"Let's not try to decide anything until Gil and Margo get here. A few more days won't make any difference. And I'm sure I don't have to warn either of you to say nothing about this. Okay?"

The next few days were all I had longed for while I was lying in that hot little room on Third Avenue. I sat in the shade with Mother; I took long walks with Eleanor and we talked about Rob and my job at Altman's. I didn't mention Third Avenue, though; I just said I'd found a small apartment, and she didn't press me for details. In the evenings I reveled in the cool breeze that sprang up, and one morning I took Eleanor's two girls with me to pick wild blueberries for Annie, who had virtually taken over in the kitchen. For the first time in many weeks I felt relaxed, restored, and ready to face the world. I was not at all prepared, however, for what happened on Friday night after Gil and Margo arrived.

They were both as excited as children on Christmas Eve about the discovery of the missing hundred thousand. I don't ever remember seeing Margo so full of animation; she was practically bubbling over.

"I just knew he'd hidden the money, Julia!" she exclaimed almost before she said hello. "Didn't I tell you? Remember when I asked you if you'd looked for the money, and you said there wasn't any?"

When at last the five of us gathered in the living room after dinner and I looked around at the faces of my brothers and their wives, I began to feel apprehensive, and to wonder what the outcome of this meeting would be. As it turned out, I did not have to wonder very long.

Rick opened the envelope and passed the bonds to Gil and

Margo so they could examine them, and then, without comment, showed them the note Father had written.

"What the hell—" Gil looked dumbfounded.

"Throw it away!" Margo was almost shouting. "We never saw it!"

"Who is this Barnes?" Gil asked. "I never heard of him."

"Yes, you did," Rick answered. "Tell them, Julia, what you told Eleanor and me."

Once more I related the story of Seth Barnes's visit to the apartment, and when I finished there was a dead silence in the room. After a moment Eleanor, who had said nothing all evening, asked if we were sure the handwriting was Father's.

"No doubt about it," Rick answered. "Well, what do we do?"

"I told you," Margo said quickly. "Throw it away, get rid of it."

"We could all use the money," Gil said. "And from what Julia said, Barnes doesn't need it."

At that point everyone seemed to talk at once:

"And he'd never know—"

"But it is his, rightfully—"

"Not anymore, it isn't."

"What harm could it do? And we need—"

"I'll die if you give it back!"

"We're the only ones who know; nothing could happen."

"It's eight thousand versus thirty-three, more with the interest—"

"Suppose he gets wind of it? We'd go to jail—"

I don't know how long the futile struggle would have gone on, the age-old struggle between good and evil, if I hadn't picked up the note to look at the handwriting once more. I was holding it a little distance away from me—I didn't have my reading glasses with me—when Margo said, "Let me see," and, leaning over, tried to snatch the note from me. The thin paper tore, and about half of it remained in my hand.

"Now look," Margo said. "It's all torn. Julia, you should have let me see it." With that, she grabbed the piece I still held, and before anyone realized what she intended to do, she whipped her cigarette lighter out of her pocket and ignited both parts of the note. We sat there in silence watching them turn to ashes in the brass bowl on the coffee table.

"It still isn't our money," I said. "At least not all of it. I think we have a right to the interest, but not—"

"Don't be silly, Julia—"

"I'm not being silly. I'm trying—"

"Well, stop."

"Can't you see it's criminal?" I asked. "The principal belongs to Barnes, but the interest was for Father, so—"

They wouldn't listen to me, and when I finally sat back and said no more, they took my silence for consent—which I guess it was, but it was grudgingly given.

After what seemed like an incredibly long time—and it was very late at night—Rick put the bonds back in the brown envelope and stood up.

"I'll take care of the distribution," he said in a low voice, and left the room.

Why I didn't refuse to take my share I don't know; I suppose it was fear of nothing but Third Avenue for the rest of my life—but I know that's no excuse.

18

After looking at several apartments in the newer buildings that had gone up in the twenties on Madison and Park avenues, I settled for a floor in a converted brownstone on East Sixty-fifth Street, the block where the Millertons and the Taylors used to live, and still a good address. The renovation had been done with care, and the attractive high-ceilinged rooms suited me perfectly.

The combination living-dining room at the rear of the house faced south and had sunlight for the better part of the day. My bedroom was not as bright, since it overlooked the street and therefore faced north, but I had no intention of spending many of my daylight hours in it anyway. Annie slept in a small room next to mine, the one that used to be known as the hall bedroom, while Patrick alternated between her bed and his own in the kitchen.

Set cunningly between the front and back rooms were the kitchen and bath; the former had a nice little ell that served as a pantry, and the latter, with its sparkling white porcelain fittings, was pure joy—a far cry from the galvanized tub under the elevated line.

Piece by piece I replaced what remained of my parents' furniture; I wanted no reminders of the months I had spent surrounded by it. I did keep the silver, however; the Audubon tea set, lovingly polished by Annie, stood on a small oval table at one side of the wood-burning fireplace, and the chest containing the flatware was kept in the pantry. I did not spend money recklessly, but shopped for bargains in the good stores, like Sloane's and Hathaway's, and by the end of October the living room was furnished to my satisfaction.

I bought dove-gray carpeting to complement the lighter gray of the walls, and built my color scheme around it. Silken folds of pale rose-colored draperies hung softly against the tall windows, and a curved sofa of a darker shade faced the fireplace, on either side of which I placed an armchair upholstered in heavy silk of a muted floral design. A refectory table at the kitchen end of the room, a small mahogany desk, and a few lamps with silk shades completed the furnishings. The whole effect was pleasing to the eye, calm and uncluttered, yet with an air of elegance, something that had been missing from my life of late.

I enjoyed coming home from a shopping trip on a rainy afternoon, sitting down with a cup of tea and a book in front of the fire that Annie would have kindled, free of worries about money. The months of poverty had left a mark, though; sometimes at night I awoke with a start, listening for the next train to rumble by, and it would be a while before I could lull myself to sleep again.

My wardrobe, too, was replenished; I bought four dinner dresses, three silks and one velvet, as well as a couple of suits and daytime dresses, along with whatever accessories seemed appropriate. I liked to change into a dinner dress in the evening—I had always done that when John was alive—and

I liked to wrap myself in my cashmere robe later on when I read for a while on the chaise in my bedroom. But all these creature comforts were not enough; something was missing, and I finally came to the conclusion that I was alone too much.

There was no longer any reason for me to remain in seclusion since I was no longer poor, and with that thought in mind I set about renewing old friendships. When I got in touch with Mary Anne Fisher, Margaret Upton, and a few other women I had known over the years, they couldn't have been nicer. Of course they knew of the reverses my family had suffered, but not one of them brought up the subject, nor did they ask any searching questions at the lunches and dinners I began to attend. I guess they simply assumed that John had left me enough to live on, and that I had been out of circulation for a while because of his death and that of my father. Rick's move to East Hampton and Gil's to California did not strike them as strange either, because a number of New York businessmen had left the city after the market crash in search of greener pastures.

It was good to be seeing old friends again, and I enjoyed being with them, but there was still a void in my life, and I was wondering how to fill it when it was suddenly filled for me.

When I returned one afternoon from the hairdresser's (what a joy it was to have my hair properly cared for again!) he was waiting at the foot of the stone steps to the house. I knew before he turned around that it was Seth Barnes, and my heart skipped a beat. My first thought was that he had somehow or other found out about about the bonds, and that I had better avoid him. It was too late, though, to cross the street and keep going; he'd seen me and was moving toward me. I was terrified, and judging from his first words, I must have looked it.

"It's all right, Mrs. Wilcox. I apologize if I startled you," he said in the quiet voice I remembered.

"What—what on earth do you want?" I asked, trying to sound as if I were in command of the situation. "I told you my father—"

"I know what you told me. But I have some things to tell you, and some questions to ask. But you're shivering; shall we go inside? Your maid refused to let me in, which is why I've been standing out here in the cold."

"Of course she wouldn't let you in; she has orders to admit no one, especially strangers. And I am not inviting you—"

"I really wish you would, Mrs. Wilcox." Again he spoke quietly, almost gently, but there was no mistaking the note of insistence in his voice. When I hesitated he put his hand lightly under my elbow and guided me up the stoop.

Annie was taken by surprise when I asked her to go out to buy some flowers and one or two other things that we didn't really need, but she was too good a servant to ask questions. She merely said that my tea was ready, and that she would bring another cup.

Barnes waited until she had left before speaking. I remained silent while I poured the tea, unsure of how much he knew or guessed. Thank goodness my hand did not shake.

"A very attractive place you have here, Mrs. Wilcox," he said, accepting the cup I held out to him. "Quite different from that apartment on Madison Avenue, and a tremendous change from the one on Third."

When I still remained silent he smiled, took a sip of tea, and put the cup down.

"Very nice indeed," he went on, letting his eyes roam around the room. "Excellent taste, and everything of the best quality. That runs into money—"

"I can't see that that is any of your affair—"

"It is, in a way," he interrupted, "and I'll tell you why. When we last met—and this may come as no surprise to you—you interested me. In fact, I was more than a little attracted to you. There's an air about you, and you have your own special brand of beauty; you must know that. A rather unusual type, and one I admire—"

"Please, Mr. Barnes—"

"No, let me finish: I want you to understand. As I was saying, I was interested in you and wanted to see you again. But you had moved by the time I went back. It took a little while to trace you, a little time, a little money."

"And just why did you want to trace me?"

"For two reasons. First, as I said, I wanted to see you; I couldn't get you out of my mind. And second, I'm curious, or you might say puzzled. When a woman suddenly gives up her job as a salesperson—oh yes, I know about your working in Altman's—and moves from a hole-in-the-wall to an expensive neighborhood, the logical conclusion is that she has come into money, had a windfall—"

"And you think I came across the hundred thousand you say you gave my father for safekeeping? Didn't my brother tell you there was no such sum?" I waited for him to nod before continuing. "Well, for your information, and I must say again that it is none of your affair, I did have a windfall. The man I was engaged to, Rob Lewiston, died tragically before we could be married, but not before he made me the principal beneficiary of his estate." At this point I stood up. "And now, if you will excuse me—"

After he left I sank back, exhausted, on the soft silken

cushions and stared unseeing at the smoldering logs. I couldn't make up my mind whether he accepted my story or not, nor could I decide whether he was more interested in recovering his money or in furthering his acquaintance with me.

19

By the end of the following week, a cold gray one in late November, it was clear that Seth Barnes intended to try to see me again; otherwise why would fresh flowers, exquisite, fragile blooms whose delicate fragrance filled my living room, arrive every other day? He had evidently not been at all deterred by his abrupt dismissal from my presence. I really ought to inquire about him, I thought, before he waylays me in the street again, or finds some other way to see me. After all, he was once a bootlegger, and could easily be involved in something illegal—

In the end I called Tom Ashcroft, John's former partner, and asked him if he knew anything about a man named Seth Barnes.

"I don't know him personally, Julia," Tom said, "but I've certainly heard of him. He's had some pretty big real estate deals in the city lately, has his own firm, and seems to be on the up and up. If he'd been in trouble with the law I'd have heard of it. Why do you want to know?"

"Oh, I met him recently; just curious, I guess," I answered. "And he's been sending me flowers—"

"Good for him," Tom chuckled. "I think he's perfectly safe, but if I hear anything I'll let you know."

I was glad I talked to Tom Ashcroft when I did, because on Saturday morning a messenger delivered a note from Seth Barnes requesting that I dine with him at the Ritz Hotel that evening.

"I noticed that you sent your maid away before we had our recent conversation," the note read in part, "and since what I have to say to you is of a private nature, I suggest dinner at the Ritz as an alternative to my visiting you. I shall call for you at seven this evening."

The messenger had evidently been told not to wait for a reply, because he clattered down the steps as soon as he had handed Annie the envelope. The nerve of Seth Barnes, I thought, the colossal nerve! He's employing the same tactics he used when he telephoned to the Madison Avenue apartment, giving me no chance to refuse. At first I was annoyed, and told Annie not to answer the doorbell when it rang at seven o'clock, but as the day wore on, something—curiosity? vanity?—made me change my mind, and by half past six I was standing in front of the full-length mirror in my bedroom, dressed in the black velvet and fastening the catch to the pearls John had given me. A new evening wrap and a pair of white kid gloves lay ready on the chaise longue. As I put a hand-embroidered handkerchief and my house key in a small velvet bag with a gold chain for a handle, I tried for the hundredth time that day to decide what the matter of a "private nature" might be: a proposal of marriage? an accusation of theft?

He couldn't, I thought, have found out about the bonds. After all, I had kept them with me from the time the mirror broke until I turned them over to Rick in East Hampton. And hadn't he said he had traced me to Third Avenue only after I had left there? Therefore he couldn't know, and the private matter must be his desire for my companionship, or possibly more than companionship, in which case I felt confident I could handle the situation.

Promptly at seven the doorbell rang, and I heard Annie asking him to wait in the living room. I think we both received a shock when we saw each other in full evening regalia; from the warm smile on his face and the way his eyes lighted up when I made my entrance I knew I was looking my best, and I must say I savored the moment. I tried not to show it, but I was almost as impressed with his appearance as he seemed to be with mine. He was impeccably turned out in what I recognized immediately as hand-tailored evening clothes, which he wore with the ease of one to whom they were no novelty. I found it difficult, though, to reconcile the image of the onetime bootlegger with that of the svelte New Yorker who guided me down the steps and handed me into the limousine that waited at the curb.

He hadn't reserved a private dining room at the Ritz, but the table to which we were shown was in such a secluded alcove that he might just as well have. He ordered for both of us, and when the solicitous waiter hurried off, Barnes leaned forward and smiled at me. I almost smiled back, forgetting for the moment the cool, distant attitude I had planned to maintain during the evening.

"If you think I'm wooing you," he said, looking me straight in the eyes, "you're right, and—"

"Mr. Barnes, if this is the private matter you spoke of, I think we'd better—"

"It's more a matter of setting the record straight," he broke in. "Whether you go on seeing me after tonight is completely up to you. There are, however, a number of things I would like you to know."

He paused while the waiter served the first course, a delicious pâté on paper-thin toast points.

"About your dealings with my father?"

"Only incidentally," he replied. "What I really want to tell you, and I realize that you are entirely unaware of any of this, is that I've actually known you ever since you were a girl—"

"But how—"

"Let me tell you. Remember the years your family spent in East Hampton? You were summer people, there to be served; we were natives, the ones who did the serving. Barneses have lived at that end of the island for generations, going back to the eighteenth century, some of them farmers, but most of them fishermen, like my father. We weren't in your class at all.

"I used to see you from time to time, as often as I could manage it, when you were there for the summer. Your family would have beach parties, clam and lobster bakes, and they'd order the shellfish from my father. I'd see to it that I delivered it, and then volunteer to prepare the fire, help the cook, anything. Your father tipped me well, but I didn't do it for that; I did it to be near you."

"I'm sorry, I don't—"

"Of course you don't remember me. I couldn't expect you to; there were too many fellows of your own crowd around. Sometimes I'd see you horseback riding with one of the Gardner boys, or you'd be walking down Main Street, and I'd follow as close as I dared. I never had the courage to speak to you. As I said, we lived in different worlds.

"Then we all grew up; I worked my way through Columbia, you came out in society and married Wilcox; I read about it in the paper. I didn't know about your engagement to Lewiston, though. That was another family we catered to, by the way."

He waited while the plates were being removed and replaced with steaming cups of consommé.

"Then we entered the war; I went into the Navy, and did my stint. When it was over I enrolled in Columbia Law School—"

"Are you a lawyer, then?"

"Half a lawyer, you might say. I was in the middle of my second year when I was forced to drop out. My father died; he drowned when a freak squall came up suddenly one afternoon. My sister had contracted infantile paralysis earlier that summer, and when Pa went, my mother, who had always been a strong woman, had a crippling stroke. So, there were two invalids to be cared for, and practically no money for doctors, nurses, medicine, treatments, and so on. You can imagine the expense."

"And that's why you turned to bootlegging?" I asked softly.

"Yes." He nodded. "Don't forget, I was a fisherman's son, and knew far more about boats than the city fellows who ran things. And as I saw it, it was the only way I could make enough money fast enough to take care of my mother and sister. Fortunately my mother never realized what I was doing, or where the money was coming from; hers was a stern puritanical nature—she would have disowned me."

"Weren't you afraid of being caught and sent to prison?" I asked.

"There wasn't much danger of that in the early days of Prohibition. The Coast Guard didn't have the manpower at first, oh, up until about 1925. Then they became much more of a threat to the rumrunners, but I was out of it by then. No, that didn't bother me; I was more worried about the mob, the racketeers. And I was right to be worried; they were after me. You see, I was not one of *them*, but I knew too much, and was therefore considered dangerous."

"Is the soup not right, Mr. Barnes?" the waiter asked anxiously, looking at my companion's untouched consommé.

"What? Oh, yes, it's fine. Just talking too much," he answered.

"You'd better have it before it cools," I said, "and let me talk."

He smiled and picked up his spoon. "Yes, do. I like to hear your voice."

"Am I right in thinking that when it became too dangerous you left the country? You said something about being followed, and that my father sent someone to pick up the money you wanted him to invest for you. I suppose that was to be for your mother and sister."

He finished his consommé and waited until the plates were removed before answering. "Yes, partly. My mother had died by that time, and I put Ruth, my sister, into a special facility for infantile-paralysis patients, down at Warm Springs. She's still there, and probably always will be. I wanted to be sure I had enough to take care of her. Yes, I needed the money for that, and also as a nest egg; I had no idea what I'd be able to do abroad, but as things turned out, I did fantastically well. I spent eight years in South Africa, where I bought an interest in a gold mine that came through. It was pleasant enough there; I liked the life, especially the time I spent in Cape Town, with its atmosphere of conservative wealth and formality. I might have stayed, but when I learned that our government had wiped out that mob, and that the ones who threatened me were dead, I knew I wanted to come home."

"Then you are perfectly safe now?" I asked, wondering if someone could still be following him.

"Not only perfectly safe," he said confidently, "but wealthy to boot. With pure gold. Rags to riches, straight out of Horatio Alger."

"Then why are you anxious to find what you *say* you gave Father for safekeeping? And why did you break into my apartment to look for the money? Or did you send someone to do it for you?"

"My God! What are you saying? Break into your apartment! If you think I'd do a thing like that—were you hurt?"

He stared at me, wide-eyed, in utter and unfeigned amazement while I described what had happened, once more forgetting to go on with his dinner.

"Look at me, my dear," he said when I finished speaking. "You asked me why I was anxious to get the money back, and I'll tell you: partly because it was so hard earned and belonged to me, but also because making inquiries about it served as an excuse to see you. But I'd never go about it by breaking into your home—that must have been a sneak thief—and frightening you. I'd cut off my right hand first; you must believe me."

I did believe him; I couldn't help it, and later on, when he talked about his childhood in East Hampton, I realized that moral values had been firmly implanted in him at an early age by a dominant mother.

"After I grew up," Seth Barnes said at one point, "I often thought she would have been completely at home in the old Massachusetts Bay Colony. When my sister and I were young, a good part of every Sunday was given over to church services and Bible reading—and how we squirmed under that discipline! My mother made very sure we were aware that the wages of sin were not only death but also eternal damnation in the fires of hell. Jonathan Edwards would have loved her. A lot of people did."

"Did you love her?" I asked when he paused. "Or did you admire her?"

"Both," he replied promptly. "She wasn't always the strict, austere, churchgoing person I've painted; she could be great fun, dreaming up treats, outings, games, and the like. There was never any too much money, but she'd manage so that we had bicycles and things the other kids had. And the feasts she'd concoct on birthdays and holidays! The religious streak never interfered with her enjoyment of the fruits of the earth."

"And your father?" I asked. "Was he like her?"

"Let's say he went along with her, to church services and suppers and all. But no, I doubt that left to himself he would have attended; you see, he worshiped her, and therefore did whatever she wanted. He was a big, taciturn man, an outdoorsman, and would far sooner have been out on the water in his boat on Sunday mornings instead of in a crowded little church listening to a sermon on the prevalence of evil in the world."

"I can't help thinking . . ." I began.

"Yes?" he said encouragingly.

"Let me put it this way: I can understand why you wouldn't want your mother to know about the bootlegging, but I can't help thinking that she would have understood."

"You're very perceptive, and you may very well be right, but I'm just as glad she didn't know. She might have blamed herself for omitting something in my early training. I'll never know, of course, but I do want you to know that I was brought up to respect morality, and that I cannot tolerate dishonesty or deceit; she did that for me."

"But weren't you dishonest, weren't you breaking the law when you sold liquor?"

"Yes, I admit that," he answered, looking steadily at me, "but you see, I wasn't doing it for myself. I felt I owed my mother and sister the best care I could provide, and at the time that was the only way I could see to do it. The end, in this case, justified the means, and I have absolutely no regrets about my actions."

* * *

As I lay in bed that night, reviewing the events of the evening, I realized that I genuinely admired the man for what he had done for his family. I couldn't imagine Rick or Gilbert risking his life to provide for Mother and me; Seth Barnes had far more strength of character than either of them, and I was beginning to be interested in furthering my acquaintance with him. My mind was at rest about the bonds; he had seemed to accept what I'd said about Rob's will, and I didn't think the subject would come up again. He'd be too afraid I'd refuse to see him.

20

I wanted to ask you to have tea with me at the Plaza this afternoon," Seth Barnes said when he phoned the next morning, "but it's snowing so hard—look, may I stop in to see you around four o'clock?"

"At least you're giving me a chance to reply this time," I said with a laugh, "instead of announcing you're coming and then hanging up."

"Very bad manners, I know," he replied. "But I was afraid—look, I'll apologize handsomely if you'll let me come."

"Very well. About four, then."

From then on I saw a great deal of him, and while I enjoyed being pursued by such an attentive—and rich—suitor, I was a little puzzled by his behavior. By his own admission he was wooing me, but as the weeks went by and he made no attempt to kiss me, or even to hold my hand, I began to wonder if just being with me, admiring my looks, taking me about, was all he wanted. Worship from afar, so to speak. He could be, I thought, one of the old school who clung to the notion that a long courtship was de rigueur before any physical contact took place. Perhaps he had inherited a share of his mother's puritanism, in which case I would just have to wait and see what developed.

I was delighted to have an escort again, instead of arriving at dinner parties by myself, and Seth seemed to fit in nicely with the group of my friends to whom I introduced him. On occasion he would give a dinner party at some restaurant for business associates, at which time he would ask me to act as hostess, or, at times, there'd be a more informal dinner in his apartment for his personal friends—not that he had too many of those, probably because he'd been abroad for so long.

Seth was, as Tom Ashcroft had said, the founder and head of a real estate and development firm, and from time to time he would tell me about the various New York properties he was buying up.

"With all the foreclosures going on, Julia, and with the state of the economy, some really splendid properties can be had for a song. Then in a few years' time they'll be worth millions," he said one evening when I asked him what happened to the town houses people could no longer afford.

"I wonder if our old house on Seventy-first Street is still occupied," I said idly.

"Would you like me to find out? Easiest thing in the world."

A few days later he reported that the family who had bought it from us had put it on the market and moved away.

"Another example of the fall of the mighty, Julia. It's happening all over the city. Bad times for those who overextended a few years ago. But that shouldn't worry you; where would you like to go to dinner tonight?"

We dined out two or three nights a week, always at one of the best restaurants, and always at a preferred table. Sometimes we'd go on to the theater, once in a while to the opera, or to a movie at the new Radio City Music Hall. On occasion, when Seth was delayed at the office, he'd ask me to meet him at the Stork Club or the Waldorf, or wherever, in which case he would send the limousine for me and I would be transported in splendor, feeling a bit regal with the fur rug tucked around me.

As I said, I was puzzled by his lack of interest in any physical contact, especially when the perfect opportunity for it arose. We were being driven up Park Avenue after seeing the Lunts and Noel Coward in the latter's startling *Design for Living*, and talking about how hugely the actors seemed to be enjoying themselves, when the chauffeur swerved suddenly to avoid a pedestrian. As the car lurched I was thrown against Seth, bumping my head on his shoulder. Instead of putting his arm around me and holding me, which would have been perfectly natural, he simply helped me to sit up again, and asked if I was all right. Oh, he was most solicitous, I couldn't complain about that, but his reluctance to embrace me made me wonder if my charms were fading, or if he was losing interest, or whether he was playing a game, the rules of which I did not understand.

I am quite sure I did not consciously plan to bring matters to a head, but that's the way things turned out. Thinking that an evening at home, dinner in the soft light of my living room, and coffee in front of the fire would be a nice change from restaurant fare, I invited Seth to dine with me the following Sunday. Annie took pains with the meal, and after what Seth pronounced a perfect Sunday-night supper (steak and kidney pie, salad, and fruit macédoine), the beaming cook retired, leaving us to linger over our coffee and the cognac

153

Seth had brought. He tended the fire, and for a while we sat comfortably, chatting about the past, about East Hampton, and how neither of us wanted to go back there. When I told him that our house there was in Mother's name and that upon her death it would be left jointly to Rick, Gilbert, and me, he was interested, and wanted to know why I didn't sell my share to Rick.

"Well, it isn't mine to sell yet," I said, "and anyway, I know he can't afford to buy me out. Besides, it doesn't matter that much to me now. It would have helped last summer, though, before I found—" I broke off abruptly.

"Found what, Julia?" he asked, looking puzzled.

"Found out I was Rob's heir," I said, hoping I spoke easily. "It was so horrible being poor, Seth, really poor; I never had any idea what it was like until then. I still dream about it at times and wake up frightened, thinking I'm still—"

I don't cry often, but at that point tears sprang into my eyes (nerves, I guess), and as I stood up to find a handkerchief, he rose and came toward me. A moment later I was in his arms, and his lips were on mine.

21

The next evening he asked me to marry him.

"Up until now I haven't dared to ask you, Julia. I've even been afraid to touch you for fear you'd turn away from me. But I think I've been in love with you forever, and I want you with me for the rest of my life. I don't want to share you with anyone—I think I'm even jealous of Annie—and there are days when I can hardly bear to have you out of my sight. I don't know how you feel about me, but you wouldn't have gone on seeing me if my company had been objectionable. So I hope—oh, my dearest, if you'll have me, you'll never want for anything. . . ."

He had come to see me after dinner that night, and we were once again in front of the fire. He held both my hands while he spoke, and kept them in his while he waited for my response, his dark eyes fastened on mine.

Perhaps that was when I fell in love with him; I'm not sure, but I am sure about one thing: that I felt miserable that I had deceived him about the bonds. He was such a good man. . . .

"I think I love you, Seth," I began, but before I could go on, his arms were around me and his lips were pressed on mine, gently at first and then with mounting passion.

"Let me finish," I begged when at length he released me. "I want to be sure that I love you, Seth, that we'll have a good marriage. Please don't rush me; I would like some time, a week at the most, so that there won't be any doubt in my mind."

Strangely enough, my not jumping at his offer seemed to please him, and as a matter of fact I did need a little time to think things out. How would my brothers react to my marrying the man they (and I) had cheated out of what was rightfully his? What would happen if I told Seth what we had done? He'd be angry, and would probably never trust me again. I had not forgotten what he said about not being able to tolerate deceit—and he would leave me. I didn't want that.

I slept badly that night, but in the morning my mind was made up: I loved Seth Barnes, and I *would* marry him, no matter what Rick and Gil said. Accordingly, after breakfast I sent Annie out to do some errands and put in a call to East Hampton. Rick was thunderstruck when I told him what I intended to do, and almost incoherent in his opposition.

"Of all things, Julia! What—what—whatever has possessed you? Keep away from Barnes! You know—my God —you'll give everything away! You'll ruin all three of us. . . ." He went on and on, and when I said there was absolutely no danger, that Seth seemed to have written the hundred thousand off as a loss, that he had millions, Rick slammed down the receiver. Two minutes later he called back, calmer, but still angry.

"Julia, listen. If you go ahead with this fool thing—and I can't stop you—be aware of this: you are in this as deeply as Gil and I are, and stand in just as much danger. I can't repay the money—it's all tied up in my office and this house. And I happen to know Gil is in no position to pay it back, not with Margo's extravagance."

"But Rick, I—"

"No, no, I haven't finished; I want you to understand that if you marry Barnes you'll be playing with fire. And if you ever breathe a word about the bonds, I'll ruin him, and ruin you. I mean what I say."

My conversation with Gil when I reached him was just as unsatisfactory, although he didn't seem as upset as Rick had sounded. Then Margo got on the phone and wanted to know if Seth Barnes was really rich. When I said yes, he was extremely wealthy, she laughed delightedly and said, "Go ahead, Julia, marry him. We could use a little wealth in this family."

I can't begin to write down all the thoughts that went through my mind during the next few days; suffice it to say that in spite of those wretched bonds, in spite of the opposition of my brothers, I knew I was in love with Seth and wanted to marry him. At the end of the week I wrote and told him that I would.

His reaction left nothing to be desired; whenever we were alone he had me in his arms, and when he wasn't kissing me, he was making one plan after another for our lives together with an almost boyish enthusiasm. If I wanted to go to Paris on our honeymoon, he would reserve a suite at the Ritz; but if I preferred Bermuda, he knew of a fully staffed house complete with private beach that he could rent. And where would I like to live afterward?

"I'll tell you what I'd really love, Seth," I said after we'd decided on Bermuda for the honeymoon. "A house, not another apartment. Nothing too grand, but large enough so that we can have a morning room, or sitting room, and a drawing room on one floor, a bedroom suite on another, and then the top floor for the maids. Oh, yes, and front and back stairs—"

"Don't forget a room to eat in," he teased.

"Oh, dear, it's beginning to sound too big; I've been thinking of something small, but elegant."

"We'll find it, dearest. There are some advantages to being in real estate. I'll get one of my men to come up with a list of possibles, and then you can see if one of them suits you. Are you really sure you don't want me to buy back your old house for you?"

"I'm positive, Seth. It wouldn't be mine. I'd feel as if it still belonged to my parents; besides, it's much larger than what I have in mind. But it's kind of you to offer."

"We'll need a summer place, too, Julia. Something within commuting distance."

I knew he was thinking of East Hampton, remembering how the husbands would arrive on the Friday-afternoon train and depart again for the city on Sunday night or Monday morning.

"Perhaps Old Greenwich would be good, Seth. A house on the water there; but we ought to take our time about that."

"Yes," he said thoughtfully, "we might want to travel in the summer if I can get away. But there will be times when I won't be able to, and I wouldn't want you stuck here in the city in the hot weather."

"Seth, what would you do if I asked you for the Taj Mahal?"

"Why, buy it for you, of course," he said with a smile. "Now stop talking and let me kiss you."

22

Shortly after our return from Bermuda I wrote to my brothers informing them of my marriage (there had been a notice in the *Times*, but I wasn't sure they would have seen it) and giving them the address of the house Seth had bought for me on East Eightieth Street. Eleanor replied at length: she was happy for me and sent her best wishes to Seth; the children, she said, were thriving; Rick was working hard; and my mother was in good health, although quite forgetful at times. Margo merely wrote a short, congratulatory note.

Seth felt that my brothers had deserted me after Father died, and couldn't understand why they left me to fend for myself.

"It strikes me as strange, Julia," he said when I gave him Eleanor's letter to read. "I remember your brothers from the early days in East Hampton; they seemed like nice fellows, a little happy-go-lucky, but decent, easygoing—"

"They were, Seth, then," I said. "And why not? They had everything they wanted, they were good-looking and popular, really sought after, and then—"

"Then when the bottom fell out of the market they found themselves in the real world. But that does not excuse them for leaving you in the lurch, Julia. I don't understand it at all."

"I do, in a way," I said. "At least I think I do. The depression changed characters as well as lives; I think it brought out the worst in some of us. When our apartment was ransacked, the police lieutenant who came said that men who had been leading perfectly blameless lives up until then were driven to crime to feed their families. Like them, Rick and Gilbert had no room in their minds for anything but the support of their families—they were almost desperate. I don't like the way they treated me, but I can understand the why of it. Besides, Seth, we were never a close family, not like yours; I think we all kept at a distance from one another, and rather selfishly, too."

"Not you, dearest. Look how you took care of Annie."

"Sometimes I think Annie took care of me," I said with a laugh, "along with Patrick. Anyway, she has repaid me in full for anything I did for her. Look at her now, how well she manages this house."

I had put her in charge of the other servants—cook, housemaid, and laundress—with the result that I hardly ever had to lift a finger. She must have been well over sixty at the time, but her energy was that of a woman half her age, and I could never persuade her to take a vacation.

She particularly enjoyed taking care of my clothes, just as she had that awful summer on Third Avenue, and she loved to have me send for her to do up the hooks on a dress if we were going out to a formal affair, and would find an excuse to stay until I had the last curl in place and the final drop of perfume on my wrist. More than once she volunteered to wait up for me "to undo all them hooks," but I had to dissuade her; Seth took great pleasure in doing that.

He also took pleasure in the dinner parties I arranged to have at home for our friends; the Cochranes, the Ashcrofts, and the Fishers were frequent guests, as well as George Duncan and John Ross (whom Seth had known at Columbia Law School) and their wives. And on one memorable occasion when Rick came to dinner—he was in the city to see a client—I rounded up a few of *his* old friends. We'd been married for almost two years at that time, and I suppose my brother had decided that by then the secret of the bonds was well buried. Or perhaps he wanted to find out what kind of man Seth was. He was evidently so well pleased with what he saw that he urged us to spend a weekend with them in East Hampton the following summer, which surprised me, but what surprised me more was Seth's ready acceptance of the invitation, and I asked him later on why he wanted to go.

"Oh, I don't know, dearest," he answered. "I guess I thought you'd like it. Perhaps we could take the ferry over from New London and just spend the day there, if you'd rather."

"What did you think of Rick?" I asked.

"Seems like a good enough fellow, but . . ."

"Yes, I know. Your opinion of him is bound to be colored by what I've told you about the past."

He nodded, and we dropped the subject then, but we did spend a pleasant day in East Hampton late in August of that year; I don't remember all the details of the visit, but I do recall that Seth was favorably impressed with Eleanor, and that Rick's oldest daughter whispered to me that she thought Seth handsome enough to be a movie star. Nice memories.

Another memory, more poignant, and at the same time painful: when I woke up one dark November morning with a sore throat and a headache, Seth was filled with concern.

"I thought you looked pale last night at the Ashcrofts'

dinner, dearest. You couldn't have felt too well," he said, putting his hand on my forehead. "Stay in bed; I'll ask Bronson to look in on you this morning. And since it's Saturday I'll knock off early, around noon, and I'll expect to find you right here, understand?"

When it turned out that I had contracted a form of influenza that Dr. Bronson said was prevalent just then, Seth insisted on my having a nurse (to Annie's dismay), and fussed over me himself until she drove him from the room. I was in bed for ten days, and when I began to feel better I asked her if I'd been delirious at any time, afraid I might have let something slip about the bonds, which shows, I suppose, how I could never completely rid my mind of them.

"No, you were never out of your senses, Mrs. Barnes," she replied. "You were sick enough, but not that sick. And a good patient, too. Another day or two and you won't be needing me, but you should take it easy for a while."

"Indeed she will," Seth said, coming into the room with a handful of travel folders. "I'm taking her south, where she can soak up some sun. Look these over, dear, when you feel up to it, and we'll decide which island to visit. And here's something I thought you'd like."

I was touched by the present he had taken the time to pick out himself (like most men he loathed shopping), and by the eager expression on his face as he watched me open it.

"You like the color, don't you?" he asked as I unfolded a beautifully embroidered peignoir of the palest Nile green. "I thought it would go with all the rosy stuff you have."

"Oh, Seth! I love it! I love it! How good of you—I can't wait to wear it!"

"Now read the card," he said, handing me an envelope. "The poet must have had someone like you in mind when he wrote this."

I smiled when I saw he had chosen a line from Herrick, one that had been familiar to me most of my life—"When as in silks my Julia goes—" and pulled his face down close to mine to hide the tears that threatened.

Perhaps it was because he was so considerate, so impossibly good to me, or maybe it was because I was in a weakened condition from my illness that all the guilt feelings in the world closed in on me that night. I lay awake long after midnight, and in a moment of despair and contrition resolved to tell him the truth about the bonds.

But in the morning, when I had better control over my emotions, I changed my mind. I couldn't risk ruining my brothers' reputations, nor could I stand the thought of losing Seth's love for me; I loved *him* too dearly for that. I knew him to be a kind and loving man, but I also knew him to be an unforgiving one, as exemplified by an incident that once took place in his office. He had asked me to meet him there one Saturday so that we'd have plenty of time for lunch before going to a matinee, and as I was early, the receptionist showed me into a small anteroom to wait. I heard the murmur of voices coming from the inner office, but could not distinguish the actual words. Then suddenly the door opened, and I could hear Seth clearly.

"No, Jackson, I will not give you another chance. You deceived me and then lied about it. No apologies or explanations can rectify that."

"But Mr. Barnes, you don't understand—"

"I understand that you have been dishonest, and that's enough."

I pretended to be deeply interested in a copy of *Town and Country* as a crestfallen young man hurried past me. Seth did not mention the incident to me, nor did I ask him about it. But I did not forget it.

163

As time went on, we settled into a routine that suited us both, spending the winter months in the city, sometimes traveling a little in the spring, and moving to our quiet retreat on the Connecticut shore for the summer. I was fond of the house we had bought on the Sound, a picturesque, old-fashioned cottage, set back far enough from the water's edge to allow for lawns and shade trees, but with an unobstructed view across to Long Island. We were both good swimmers, and if the tide was right we would sometimes bathe early, before breakfast; but more often Seth preferred to swim in the late afternoon when he came up from the city, after which we would relax on the padded chairs on the terrace with long cool drinks and watch the sunset. Or, if he came home early enough and it wasn't too hot, we'd play a few games of tennis at the nearby club and swim afterward.

I look back on those years rather wistfully now, thinking of how confidently I expected them to go on and on. They did, for a while, and then in the spring of 1938 Margo and Gil moved back to New York.

23

The moment I heard that my brother and sister-in-law were returning to the city, I began to feel uneasy, although for no reason that I could put my finger on. Gil had not lost his job; he was merely being transferred to the New York office, so there was no cause for worry on that score. Margo was happy about the move, Seth was interested in meeting them both, and Eleanor was making plans for a family reunion in East Hampton.

"As you know, Julia," she said when I called to ask about Mother's health, "we have plenty of room for everyone. And won't it be wonderful to have the whole family together again?"

I tried to sound enthusiastic, but the thought of the six of us gathered around the coffee table in that living room conjured up the image of the burning note, and I found it difficult to shake off a wave of foreboding that swept over me.

I needn't have worried; the reunion over the Memorial Day weekend went off without incident. The weather was perfect, everyone was in good spirits, Mother thought the celebration was in her honor, and I was able to banish any apprehension I had felt. Seth drove me over to see the little house with the brown shingles in which he had grown up, and then down to the dock from which his father had launched his fishing boat, and from which we could see where the lobster pots used to be.

"It all seems so long ago, Julia," he said as we strolled along the edge of the water. "Another world, and a good one, but—"

"But what, Seth?"

"This one's better," he said with a smile and put his arm around my shoulders. "In that one you were beyond my reach. See that rock over there? That's where I used to sit and think about you."

I reached up and drew his face down to mine, and he held me close to him until the shriek of a sea gull startled us both. I like to think about that morning.

It wasn't until we were back in New York that I realized that I wasn't the only one at the reunion who had been concerned about stirring up memories; someone, either Rick or Eleanor, had seen to it that the brass bowl that had contained the ashes of Father's note was removed from the coffee table. I wondered if Margo or Gil had noticed.

In June we moved, as usual, up to the cottage on the Sound, and we hadn't been there more than a few days when Margo called and asked if she and Gil could come for a weekend.

"We can't afford a summer place, Julia," she said, "and my family's farm is gone now. Will you be an angel and take us in? You know what weekends in the city can be like in the summer."

I had no idea, when I said yes, of course, we'd be delighted, that one weekend would lead to another, but that's what happened. They were frequent guests that summer, and at first I rather enjoyed having them. Seth didn't seem to mind; he liked playing tennis with Gil, and Margo amused him with her chatter and her obvious interest in him.

"I think you've made a conquest, Seth," I said teasingly one Sunday night after they'd left. "Did you notice how Margo was trying to cuddle up to you last night when you were sitting on the sofa?"

"Yes," he said, "I did. And did *you* notice how quickly I got up and pulled you down on the love seat next to me?"

"You'd better be careful," I said lightly. "You know what they say about a woman scorned." I did not feel particularly lighthearted, though, and I was glad our guests were going to East Hampton the following weekend.

It was late in August when things began to go wrong. Margo and Gil came up from the city with Seth on Friday afternoon in time for a swim before dinner, and after the meal we went out onto the terrace for coffee. I know now that that was when Seth's suspicions were first aroused.

Gil was saying something about the steaming pavements in the city when Margo interrupted him.

"Oh, was it ever hot!" she exclaimed. "I thought I'd faint away on Fifty-ninth Street one day. Oh, that reminds me, Julia; I ran into one of our mutual friends that day. Remember Ellen Lewiston? You were at school with her, weren't you? She married one of the Briggs boys and moved to Boston, you know. I was so surprised to see her; I went into this bookstore on Fifty-ninth, where they had a book on modern dance in the window, and there she was. She owns the place! Remember her brother, Rob? Apparently he died and left it to her. She said it was a godsend, because she and her husband lost so much in '29. They moved back here, and now they're running the business. You ought to stop in and see her, Julia. She'd be delighted."

I felt the blood draining away from my head during this recital and wondered if I was going to faint. Seth glanced at me, but he said nothing until we were on our way to bed.

"Didn't you say Lewiston had left his estate to you, Julia?" he asked, frowning slightly. "That's what I understood you to say."

"Yes, you understood correctly," I answered, feeling a cold sweat break out on my palms. "Rob's lawyer called me and said I had inherited the money; nothing was said about the bookstore, though." I paused, and tried to smile ruefully. "I guess I confused his money—although it was not a tremendous amount—with his estate. I'm glad Ellen has the store, though. She's the kind of person to make a go of it."

I can't put into words the relief I felt when he said he was just as glad that I wasn't running a bookstore and turned off the light on the night table.

24

I thought that was the end of the matter, that Seth had accepted my explanation, and that he would not refer to it again. He did not mention it, but I noticed that for most of the rest of the weekend he seemed preoccupied. I assumed he had business affairs on his mind; he'd been unusually busy that summer, not only with his own office, but with a housing commission that Mayor La Guardia had asked him to head up. I think I was partly right, for when Gil asked him if his work with the commission would lead to a political appointment, Seth said he thought it might, and that he was considering turning over most of his private business to an associate and devoting himself to fair and proper housing for the poorer segment of the population. He couldn't handle both, he said.

"Could you find us a luxury apartment on Park or Fifth for a pittance, Seth?" Margo asked in a coaxing sort of way.

"If you didn't spend half my salary on yourself, we could afford Park Avenue," Gil said crossly. "You can't have both."

"Julia has both," pouted Margo. "I can't see why——"

"Shut up, Margo." Gil rose from the deck chair where he'd been lounging in the late-afternoon sun.

"I won't shut up," she cried, "and if you're not careful I'll tell—oh-oh!" She gasped as Gil slapped her across the cheek. She stood for a moment, tears streaming down her face, and then turned and fled into the house. Gil waited until she was inside, then slowly followed her.

We managed to get through the rest of the weekend without another scene, but the atmosphere was strained; I was relieved when it was over, and we had the cottage to ourselves. I was not anxious to see Margo again, and I didn't for a few weeks. After our return to the city in early September Seth was so busy, coming home late, and working all day Saturday, that we did no entertaining at all. Then Rick called and begged us to go down to East Hampton to celebrate Eleanor's birthday on the twenty-first of the month.

"I owe her a treat, Julia, but when I asked her if she'd like a night on the town she said no, that what she really wanted was a family party here with champagne and a Lady Baltimore cake, whatever that is. You and Seth will come, won't you?"

I said I would certainly be there, and that I would provide the cake, but I wasn't sure about Seth.

"He's so busy, Rick," I said. "I've never known him to work such long hours. It's all this housing business the mayor has him doing, meeting after meeting. But I will ask him."

I was asleep when Seth came in that night, and he looked tired at breakfast the next day. I was sure he'd say he couldn't spare the time to go to East Hampton, but when I mentioned it he looked thoughtful for a moment, and then to my surprise said he'd like to go.

"I'll make time, Julia. I'm pretty sure I'll be able to, so tell them we'll be there." And he hurried off without kissing me good-bye, which was not like him at all.

On the morning of the twenty-first, however, he phoned me from the office saying he'd be delayed.

"You take the train, Julia, and I'll drive down later. I'll probably get away from here between four and five, and get there sometime before ten."

We had had unusually heavy rains for two or three days—equinoctial storms, I think the papers said—and when I left New York, the air was heavy and humid under a gray sky. Margo and Gil, who had expected to drive down with us, took the train with me, and seemed rather listless and out of sorts, perhaps because of the weather. I don't know. They made an effort, though, at the birthday dinner, and Rick was in such a happy mood, popping champagne corks and urging everyone to drink up, that the party became quite lively.

It was not until we were in the living room, drinking brandy from the large snifters Father had used so often, that Seth arrived. As he entered the room a sudden gust of wind blew the door to the terrace shut so hard that one of the small panes of glass shattered, startling us all. But what startled me even more was the grim, unsmiling expression on my husband's face as he looked from one to the other of us.

"Come in, come in," Rick said heartily. "Whew, what a night! The barometer's way down. Come on, Seth, make yourself comfortable. You've missed out on the champagne, but we're still celebrating with brandy, and there's plenty of it."

"I don't think you'll go on celebrating," Seth said in a low, controlled voice. "Not when you hear what I have to say."

"What the hell—" Gilbert began.

"Seth, what is it? What is wrong?" I asked.

"Plenty," he answered, without looking at me. "And I'll tell you. . . ." I couldn't hear the rest of what he said because what sounded like a chair or table being blown over on the terrace made such a noise. Eleanor glanced nervously at the windows, but the rest of us simply stared at Seth.

"Sit down, all of you," he said in a commanding tone I had never heard him use. "And listen to me."

"Goddamn it, I will not be ordered about in my own house," Rick shouted. His voice sounded strange, thick, and I realized he'd had far more than usual to drink, what with the pre–dinner cocktails, the champagne, and then the brandy.

"Suit yourself," Seth muttered, taking some folded papers out of an inner pocket. I remember looking at the others and seeing Eleanor's puzzled expression and Margo's frightened one. Rick looked belligerent, and I was suddenly afraid he might lose control and turn ugly.

"It's taken me a while," Seth began, "to put the evidence together, but I have it now, right here." He tapped the papers he held. "All the evidence I need to prove that the three of you, Rick, Gil, and you, Julia, knowingly and willfully conspired to steal the sum of one hundred thousand dollars that I gave to your father to hold in safekeeping for me."

"How—" Gil stopped short.

"I'll tell you how. Mr. Hastings *did* keep the money safe, although when I first talked to Julia and saw the conditions under which she'd been living I was convinced he'd lost it in the Stock Market and decided to say nothing about it."

He paused, and I expected him to look at me, but he kept his eye on Rick.

"That's what I thought at first. Then Margo mentioned Lewiston's bookstore, and how his sister had inherited it. Julia lied to me; Lewiston didn't leave her any money. His will is on file in the probate court, and everything went to his sister, Ellen Lewiston Briggs. So where did Julia's sudden wealth come from?"

No one answered him.

"That was the first clue I had. Then Margo, in a fit of temper, made a slip, threatening to 'tell' something that was so secret, so important, that Gil struck her to stop her. That led me to investigate further, and I found that Richard Hastings and Gilbert Hastings, who were known to be hard hit by the depression, had made substantial deposits in August 1931, at the same time that a similar amount was deposited to Julia's account."

He paused again, still ignoring me.

"And I *will* have that money repaid, if I have to take you to court. You've abused my hospitality, made a monkey out of me, and now—"

"You take this to court and I'll ruin you," Rick cried. "How would you like your political friends to know you were a common bootlegger and that that's where the money came from?"

"I have no worry on that score. The mayor knows my life story. But there's more." And he glanced at Margo. "Your wife, Gil, approached me with a proposition. In return for my finding her a Park Avenue apartment for practically nothing, she would tell me what happened to a certain sum of money. Here's her letter—no, wait, I must have left it in my briefcase in the car. Stay there." And he went quickly to the front door.

"Margo, what in the name of time did you do?" Rick was yelling now.

"Don't let him get my letter," she wailed, but Gil was already running out of the house after Seth. I don't know what he intended to do, tear up the letter, maybe. Rick had just started after him when there was a thunderous crash, as if part of the chimney had fallen onto the roof, and then the lights went out.

"Candles," Rick shouted. "Eleanor, where's the flashlight? Where—"

"Help! Help me!" Gil's hoarse voice came from the doorway. "A tree fell on the car! Seth's pinned—"

I flew out of the house and ran toward the driveway. In the darkness I could just make out the shape of the car under a mass of branches and leaves, and then I was tugging at a limb that was in my way when Gil called me.

"Over here, Julia, this side—"

I followed his voice and saw that the door on the driver's side of the car was open, but I couldn't see Seth. I was trying to climb over the huge trunk of the tree when something struck me across the back and a fierce pain ran up my spine. A moment later I was lifted off my feet and thrown to the ground. The last thing I heard before losing consciousness was Gil saying "Oh my God, oh my God," over and over again.

25

I cannot help but wonder if Seth had some premonition of death before he went down to East Hampton that night; I think he may have had, because less than a week before that, he made a new will, leaving the bulk of his fortune to foundations engaged in the search for a vaccine for the prevention of infantile paralysis. He also instructed his executor to press charges against Rick and Gil if they did not willingly pay to his estate what they stole from him.

I was forgiven my debt, and I tried to help my brothers —by selling my jewels and a few other valuables—but still they had to borrow heavily.

They had a dreadfully hard time, and, not too surprisingly, Margo left Gil. She married a wealthy importer of furs, but he divorced her after a few years and we don't know where she is now. Rick, who was blinded in one eye by flying debris the night of the storm, is still eking out a living in East Hampton. I do not see him very often; Eleanor and he come into the city infrequently, and the trip to the country is too much for me now.

The hurricane that killed Seth, one of the worst storms of the century, left me crippled. They tell me that I was almost electrocuted by a live wire that fell on me, and that I'm lucky to be alive. I'm not so sure about that: my legs are paralyzed from a spinal injury, and I get around only in a wheelchair or on crutches.

Seth did not disinherit me; he left me a modest income, enough so that I can afford this little apartment on Lexington Avenue, just above Bloomingdale's. And I have Annie, dear faithful Annie, to look after it and me. She's getting on in years now, and should be pensioned off, but she won't hear of it. I think she's worried, too, that I will outlive her and not be able to find anyone to take care of me, but judging from the way I've been feeling lately, that may not be the case.

Sometimes when I think of the men I loved—and who loved me—and how they all met with violent deaths, I have to wonder whether I shall be held responsible for what happened to them. There was nothing I could have done to stop the boat that killed John, or the car that ran over Rob, of that I am sure. But Seth—if only I'd told him about the bonds, if only I'd been honest with him, he'd be alive with me today. Or would he have left me? I don't know, but I do know that in some awful, fateful way I brought disaster to all three of my lovers, and now it seems that retributive justice is being meted out to me. Is there, I wonder, such a thing as doing a painful penance on earth instead of in whatever afterworld awaits us? Or am I never to have the peace of mind I long for?

Nights can be bad, especially when the pain in my back prevents sleep, but it's easy enough to get through the days. In the morning I go across the hall and read the newspaper to an elderly woman whose sight is failing, and often in the afternoons friends come to see me. Grace Cochrane and Mary Anne Fisher are particularly loyal, and Ellen comes too, bringing me books, just as Rob used to. And Gil is here for dinner fairly often. He and I are closer now than we ever were, and I am glad of that. In spite of the disfiguring burn scars on his face—a result of his trying to pull me out from under the wire that fell on me—he's cheerful enough. He was absolutely crushed when Margo deserted him, but he's over that now. At least he can talk about her without becoming emotional, and he often does. One night recently he told me something that surprised me, although perhaps it shouldn't have.

"You didn't know, did you, Julia," he said as he wheeled me into the living room after dinner, "that Margo was responsible for the break-in at the Madison Avenue apartment? She wanted that money so badly, and she was convinced that Father had it hidden away there. She got hold of a dancer she knew, an acrobatic dancer who was out of work, and promised him a share—I don't know how much—if he could find it.

"They waited until they thought you'd be sleeping; she didn't know Annie was back. Then she showed him how to go up on the dumbwaiter. He had to try it twice; the first time he got cold feet, but she persuaded him to try it again. He was to make it look like a robbery, so he took some spoons. The poor guy sprained his ankle when the rope broke and the dumbwaiter fell, and he couldn't have danced even if he'd had a job. Margo thought the whole thing was a lark. Of course she didn't tell me about it until long afterward."

So that was what came of her "snoopin'." Somehow that doesn't seem to matter much now. What does matter is my inability to rid my mind of the past; I don't know how many times during the last ten years I have relived the horrors of the night of Eleanor's birthday. Sometimes I dream about them, and then when I wake up I am invariably reminded of the last act of *Götterdämmerung*—the fury of the storm, I suppose, taking the place of the fire and flood in Wagner's great work. Ironically enough, that was one of Seth's favorite operas; he loved the grandeur of it, and we heard it at the Met several times. In a way, I can see a parallel between what happened to the gold of the Rhine Maidens, which spelled tragedy for those who stole it, and the hundred thousand dollars, which brought pain and suffering to us, who had no right to it.

I wonder how much longer . . .

Gilbert R. Hastings
223 East 76th Street
New York, N.Y.

July 8, 1952

Mrs. William Briggs
Lewiston's Bookshelf
129 East 59th Street
New York, N.Y.

Dear Ellen,

Thanks for sending me Julia's notebooks. A good part of what she wrote was, naturally, familiar, but other sections were totally new to me, like the bit about Third Avenue—we never heard about that.

I wouldn't want the manuscript made public right now, but I am thinking of instructing the executor of my will to take steps toward its publication in 1975 or 1980, when everyone concerned will be long gone. No one will be hurt that way.

Perhaps I'll see you and Bill in East Hampton when I go down to visit Rick and Eleanor. In the meantime, thanks again, Ellen, and all best wishes.

Gil